NO MERCY

(A Valerie Law FBI Suspense Thriller —Book One)

BLAKE PIERCE

Blake Pierce

Blake Pierce is the USA Today bestselling author of the RILEY PAGE mystery series, which includes seventeen books. Blake Pierce is also the author of the MACKENZIE WHITE mystery series, comprising fourteen books; of the AVERY BLACK mystery series, comprising six books; of the KERI LOCKE mystery series, comprising five books; of the MAKING OF RILEY PAIGE mystery series, comprising six books; of the KATE WISE mystery series, comprising seven books; of the CHLOE FINE psychological suspense mystery, comprising six books; of the JESSE HUNT psychological suspense thriller series, comprising twenty four books; of the AU PAIR psychological suspense thriller series, comprising three books; of the ZOE PRIME mystery series, comprising six books; of the ADELE SHARP mystery series, comprising fifteen books, of the EUROPEAN VOYAGE cozy mystery series, comprising four books; of the new LAURA FROST FBI suspense thriller, comprising nine books (and counting); of the new ELLA DARK FBI suspense thriller, comprising eleven books (and counting); of the A YEAR IN EUROPE cozy mystery series, comprising nine books, of the AVA GOLD mystery series, comprising six books (and counting); of the RACHEL GIFT mystery series, comprising six books (and counting); of the VALERIE LAW mystery series, comprising three books (and counting); and of the PAIGE KING mystery series, comprising three books (and counting).

An avid reader and lifelong fan of the mystery and thriller genres, Blake loves to hear from you, so please feel free to visit www.blakepierceauthor.com to learn more and stay in touch.

GIRL, HUNTED (Book #3)
GIRL, SILENCED (Book #4)
GIRL, VANISHED (Book 5)
GIRL ERASED (Book #6)
GIRL, FORSAKEN (Book #7)
GIRL, TRAPPED (Book #8)
GIRL, EXPENDABLE (Book #9)
GIRL, ESCAPED (Book #10)
GIRL, HIS (Book #11)

LAURA FROST FBI SUSPENSE THRILLER
ALREADY GONE (Book #1)
ALREADY SEEN (Book #2)
ALREADY TRAPPED (Book #3)
ALREADY MISSING (Book #4)
ALREADY DEAD (Book #5)
ALREADY TAKEN (Book #6)
ALREADY CHOSEN (Book #7)
ALREADY LOST (Book #8)
ALREADY HIS (Book #9)

EUROPEAN VOYAGE COZY MYSTERY SERIES
MURDER (AND BAKLAVA) (Book #1)
DEATH (AND APPLE STRUDEL) (Book #2)
CRIME (AND LAGER) (Book #3)
MISFORTUNE (AND GOUDA) (Book #4)
CALAMITY (AND A DANISH) (Book #5)
MAYHEM (AND HERRING) (Book #6)

ADELE SHARP MYSTERY SERIES
LEFT TO DIE (Book #1)
LEFT TO RUN (Book #2)
LEFT TO HIDE (Book #3)
LEFT TO KILL (Book #4)
LEFT TO MURDER (Book #5)
LEFT TO ENVY (Book #6)
LEFT TO LAPSE (Book #7)
LEFT TO VANISH (Book #8)
LEFT TO HUNT (Book #9)

PROLOGUE

There was one patient Doctor Mason Winters feared more than any other.

As the clock ticked on the wall of the doctor's claustrophobic office, his anxiety and apprehension grew with each movement of its hands.

The hour was coming.

It was time to face the patient he dreaded most, yet again.

Leaving his office and locking the door behind him, the doctor's keys echoed along the narrow, sterile corridor. He glared at the clipboard in his hands. It contained recent updates about the patient's condition, including notes from their previous conversations.

Those conversations had not gone well.

The patient enjoyed remembering his terrible crimes, but he took equal pleasure in withholding information.

This gave him power. He would often mock the medical staff by mimicking their voices, making them say the most horrendous things. Sometimes he delighted in this, sometimes he seemed distant and confused.

He was the epitome of a fractured, unpredictable personality.

Sighing, Doctor Winters looked once more at his clipboard of notes with displeasure and then walked down the corridor towards Ward 11's front desk.

He immediately saw that things were not as they should have been.

Looking around, there was no one at the large white desk that sat in front of the locked entrance to the ward. One of the security guards by the name of Larry Makin should have been there to greet him with that cigar-stained, yellow smile of his.

He wasn't there. The desk was empty.

Doctor Winters knew Larry liked to bend the rules, but this was unacceptable. All doctors were to be accompanied by at least one security personnel when visiting violent patients. While Larry was often late for work and had a bad habit of making inappropriate jokes towards female members of the staff, he was always out front when it

1

came to the evening sessions. To be AWOL for that would not be tolerated by the institute.

Something then caught the doctor's attention.

He leaned over the front of the sterile white desk. A row of eight monitors displayed grainy footage from various security cameras throughout Ward 11. They cycled repeatedly, showing the corridor running through the heart of the ward and then the secured rooms of each patient. As the screens switched between cameras, one showed nothing but an impenetrable black with some static interference.

Doctor Winters knew what should have been on that screen.

It should have shown a man capable of the most barbaric, brutal violence, either sleeping soundly in his bed or waiting for Doctor Winters's visit. But it did not; there was just blackness with occasional wisps of static.

The doctor hoped that Larry was absent because he was just checking the camera.

Reaching down, he pulled his radio off his belt.

"Larry, where are you?" he said into the receiver.

"Where are *you*?" Larry replied quickly over static.

"God dammit, Larry. I'm where I should be. At the front desk. Are you taking a leak again?"

"I wish." The radio buzzed momentarily. "There's a problem with one of the cameras inside room 16."

Doctor Winters sighed with relief. "I can see that on the monitor."

"Yeah," came Larry's gruff voice over the radio. "I've got a tech guy coming down here, but my supervisor said I should keep an eye on the room until he arrives."

"That's fine," the doctor said. "I'm on my way."

He flicked the switch on Larry's desk to release the lock on the metal security doors. The internal lock clicked, echoing out.

Winters looked down at the pressing questions typed on a sheet of glaring yellow paper. The first question read:

"Where is Anne Marlin's body?"

Another pointless question that the patient would never answer unless a personal connection could be made. And yet the doctor still had to ask it.

It was his job.

The FBI were breathing down the institute's already controversial neck for more information. Doctor Winters understood their desire to connect the patient to a large number of cold cases, but the patient had given him practically nothing in countless sessions. The FBI didn't seem to understand the difficulty in making a highly manipulative psychopath talk.

Composing himself for the inevitable car wreck that the interview would be, he pulled the metal security door open and stepped inside the ward.

The door automatically closed behind him, locking in place. It clicked with another echo. He had gotten used to the way sound would bounce around that locked ward, but it still made him uneasy with each visit.

The echo traveled down the clinically white ward corridor, beset on all sides by sixteen rooms with sixteen equally silent white doors. There was always an unearthly quality to that sound as it echoed and then suddenly stopped dead.

It was strange that the second security guard, who was usually posted inside the ward, was absent. Doctor Winters nearly spoke this thought out loud. He had a habit of talking to himself when he was alone, but he had managed to avoid doing it when anyone else was within earshot since coming to the institute. It wouldn't have gone down well if one of the psychiatrists was seen having a conversation with himself.

He was right, however; there should have been another security guard on duty inside the ward, but the doctor couldn't see him. In fact, he couldn't see Larry, either.

The long corridor showed only closed doors.

Doctor Winters clicked the talk button on his radio.

"Larry, where are you, and where the hell is the other guard?"

"We've got a problem, Doc," Larry said, breathing heavily over the static. "Our patient here thought he'd be clever and lunge at me while I was taking a look at the security camera in his room."

"Larry, for crying out loud," said the doctor. "Leave that to the IT guys!"

"I thought I could fix it. I've got a camera at home. Mine usually just needs a good smack and it's right as rain. I tried…"

More static made the rest of Larry's sentence impossible to decode. The cells on Ward 11 were surrounded by three feet of thick concrete. The radios always struggled to get through.

The doctor sighed, but this time he didn't hit the talk button on his radio. Instead, he just grumbled. "I'm surrounded by the Marx Brothers."

More static.

"…later on. Can you sedate this chump?" Larry said, breathing even more heavily over the radio. "It's taken both of us to hold him down."

"Yeah, I'll be right there."

Winters knew which room belonged to the patient. It was the last door on the ward and the one he dreaded the most. Each time he visited it for a wellness check or therapy session, he dreaded that the patient would be awake and ready to talk. If he was, then he would be waiting for the doctor with a smiling face. Then the conversation would begin, and what that man liked to talk about made Mason Winters PhD's head spin. The man never spoke of his crimes, but he did speak in fragments, equally violent and disturbed. Cryptic pieces came to the man's mind like black confetti, raining down all around him.

Either he was the most clinically insane person Doctor Winters had ever encountered or he was so brilliant, he'd pulled the wool over everyone's eyes with an impeccable performance.

The radio buzzed again. "Hurry," Larry said.

Looking down, the doctor tore off the piece of yellow paper with designated questions, scrunched it up and put it in his pocket. He then rushed down the corridor at speed, fumbling for a hypodermic needle and his small bottle of lorazepam in his coat pocket. It was always a good idea to carry a sedative when surrounded by such violent patients.

As he ran down the corridor, Doctor Winters felt relieved at knowing that he wouldn't have to push those pointless questions on the patient that night.

But maybe he could calm the man down.

Maybe he could offer him an olive branch and frame himself in a more positive light than the security guards. Good doctor, bad guards. Maybe then, the doctor would finally have his trust and be able to help him.

About halfway down the hallway, he saw something against the stark white of the floor. It was a tiny spec of red, and it was enough to stop him in his tracks. Leaning over, he reached out to touch it, but before he could, a voice spoke. It was indistinct and whispered. The words were unsure, an uncertain jumble, but they were real, nonetheless.

Doctor Winters stood up. "Hello?" he said, loudly.

Now it was his own voice that echoed in that strange, cavernous way that was only experienced in Ward 11.

4

No reply was given.

He nervously grabbed at his radio.

"Larry, are you there?"

The radio remained silent.

That was enough for Winters; he was going to sound the alarm regardless of whether he would be reprimanded for it later.

Stepping over to the wall, there was a red metal circle with a small yellow handle at the center. He reached out to yank the handle down, but before his fingertips could touch it, a voice spoke again. This time over the radio, and the words were louder and more certain.

"Doctor Winters," a voice said among the static. But it certainly wasn't Larry's "Sorry... Had to restrain the patient. He just went crazy."

"Is that..." Doctor Winters's question was cut off abruptly.

"Gary Jenkins, Doctor. Could you help me with Larry? He's hurt."

Doctor Winters knew Gary's name; he was a newer guard who had been working on the ward for a couple of weeks.

"Hurry, Doctor!"

Doctor Winters's desire to help Larry now took over. He may have been tardy and unreliable, but the doctor had grown fond of him, even if he was only just now admitting this to himself.

The doctor moved quickly down the corridor and came to the final door, the last room on the ward: the patient's room and the place he dreaded most.

The door had appeared to be shut, from a distance, but once he was standing in front of it, hypodermic needle now in hand and brimming with a tranquilizer, he could see that the door was very slightly ajar.

Reaching out, he dropped his clipboard and pushed the heavy white metal door open a little more, just enough to take in the terrible scene.

What he saw turned his stomach.

The floor was smeared in thick red blood. It looked like a slaughterhouse. Larry was on the ground. His body was covered in stab wounds, the remains smeared in blood. Doctor Winters only knew it was him from the name tag on his chest.

A second body lay next to him, no doubt Gary Jenkins. The young man's throat had been slit.

Winters's first reaction was to vomit, but panic set in, stopping him from throwing up.

As he stood there in the hallway, rooted to the spot in panic, a terrifying question managed to break free from the cacophony of racing

5

thoughts in his mind: Where was the patient?

"Good evening, Doctor," a low, whispered voice said over the radio. "I've been so looking forward to our talk."

Doctor Winters's hand shook as he reached for his radio, ready to call in the emergency. But as he touched it, something grabbed his attention. The sight of it made him break out in a cold sweat, his legs frozen in place and his heart beating irregularly.

Someone was hiding behind the door. They were peering through the open hinge, intently.

The doctor knew the look of that glaring eye. He knew its dispassionate, cold brutality. He knew its twisted fantasies. He knew what it was capable of.

The patient was still in the room. Just inches away. Studying him.

"Help me, Doc, help me," the voice behind the door said, mimicking almost exactly, the voice of poor Gary Jenkins. The young man with his eyes torn out on the floor.

"Yeah, Doc," the voice said, now twisting into the gruff tones of Larry. "We're hurt so bad. Help us..."

Winters knew that the patient could warp his voice to mimic him and the other doctors, but he had underestimated the man's abilities. This was frighteningly note perfect.

Then a laugh came, a sneering, gloating cackle, and it echoed with grim hopelessness against the sterile walls of Ward 11.

Winters fumbled with the radio, but then the eye moved from the other side of the door. The figure behind it leaped out and grabbed at the doctor's hand, wrenching the radio from his grip and then smashing it against the floor.

Winters watched it crack down the side on impact, its lights going out.

He then remembered the syringe.

He lifted his hand, shaking so bad he could barely hold it, and held it before his face as if it were a shield.

"DOCTOR!" the patient screamed.

It startled him so much; he wasn't expecting the patient to strike so quickly again. A hand and fingers clawed down the doctor's face drawing blood. He let out a gasp, but this only spurred on his attacker.

The doctor reeled backwards, the blood from above his eyes obscuring his vision.

A bloodied figure moved forward towards him.

Then, the syringe was gone, as if the shadows themselves had plucked them from his grasp.

He was defenseless

The patient roared with laughter.

Escape possessed the doctor, overpowering and primal. He had to run for his life. He turned and rushed back along the corridor to the security door as fast as he could.

This time his footsteps didn't echo in the emptiness. This time, they were joined by another set of footsteps.

Close behind.

He glanced back through bloodied tears to see the shape of the patient right behind him, arm outstretched.

As Winters reached the keypad beside the security door, he fumbled for his ID, swiping it through and then punching in the necessary numeric pass code.

The internal lock clicked, and the door opened.

"Thank you, Doctor Winters," an erratic, guttural voice said into the Doctor's ear. "It's the lights in here… They hurt my eyes… I wonder if it's raining outside… I don't like the water…. Do you think the people on the outside will be happy to see me? Don't… Don't answer. I want to see their faces."

The doctor felt the patient's breath creeping into his ear and spilling down his cheek and to his nose. The smell was foul. The words confused and ranting.

Panic rushed through the doctor's veins, carried by his struggling heart.

He pulled at the door and let out a whimper.

"I... I just want to help you...," was all he could say, his voice quivering like a scared child's.

Then he felt it.

Two powerful hands wrapped themselves around the doctor's throat from behind.

"You have helped me, Doctor. Now let me help you."

Out of the corner of his eye, he saw a wide, manic smile.

As Doctor Mason Winters lost consciousness, he prayed that his death would not be as painful as the two dead security guards had endured.

The last thing he heard was his killer's ice-cold words:

"Don't worry, Doctor Winters. You won't be alone… I'll kill them all."

CHAPTER ONE

The cellphone by her bed sprung into life playing "Run, Baby, Run" by Sheryl Crow.

Valerie loved and hated that song. It reminded her of being a kid, and those were not happy memories. And yet she chose to relive them each time someone called. A penance for a family sin she relived in her head every day.

"You don't start work for a couple of hours," her boyfriend Tom groaned from the other side of the bed.

Valerie didn't need to look at the screen. She knew who was calling. It could only be one person. And it could only mean one thing.

She opened her eyes to the blurry early morning in her apartment bedroom and picked up the phone.

"Agent Law?" the voice said on the other line.

"Yes, Sir," Valerie answered, trying to sound as alert as possible. She didn't completely pull this off.

"I know you're scheduled for 9 AM today, but can you get in sooner? It's a matter of great urgency."

Valerie's heart sank.

That meant no long shower and no time to force down her breakfast, either. She was going to have to face whatever *this* was still feeling less than human.

"No problem," she said, sitting up and sliding her feet into her fleece slippers next to her bed. "I take it, it's a priority case then?"

"Yes," said the voice. "But this one is different, Law. Your recent performance has warranted this. There's more going on, but I'll brief you when you arrive at HQ."

"Got it." Valerie hung up the phone and felt her empty stomach lurch a little.

What did he mean by my recent performance?

The last thing Valerie needed was uncertainty in her career. But could it have been something else? Was she being pushed aside because of what she did on the last case?

"No time for breakfast?" Tom asked groggily.

"Sorry, Honey," she replied.

"Have you thought any more about last night?"

Standing up, Valerie walked to her closet and pulled out a black pressed suit. Moving over to a drawer, she opened it and grabbed her ID and her Glock 5. It was standard issue with the FBI, and although she preferred a larger caliber than a 9mm, it had proved its worth several times over. It had to when you were in the business of chasing fugitives.

"We can talk about last night later when we have more time."

"You never have time."

"That's not true. I love being with you, but I just want us to get the timing right, okay?"

She walked back to the bed, leaned over and gave Tom a peck on the cheek.

Tom got out of bed and pulled on his jeans and white top from the previous night, saying little.

"Tom, don't be like…"

"It's fine…," he said, sighing. "You're worth waiting for. You want me to rustle you up some eggs or something before you go?"

"I'll grab something at work when I get a chance." Valerie rubbed her forehead and winced slightly.

"We shouldn't have had those Mojitos last night," Tom laughed. "You hit it pretty hard. That's not like you on a weeknight."

Valerie smiled, but inside she knew why she'd drank so much. She knew something Tom didn't.

It had been her mother's birthday.

Another year gone by without seeing her; another year of keeping her family's secret.

*

The office door in front of her read "Deputy Assistant Director Weller."

Weller was a good boss, one of the best in the FBI's Mesmer Building in Quantico, but he was tough on his agents if he had to be. Valerie was wary of that, especially considering what had happened on the last case.

Jackson could be your guardian angel or your worst nightmare.

Raising her hand, Valerie clenched her fist ready to knock, but the door opened before she could.

A smiling brown face with black hair, brown eyes, and a strong jaw was there to greet her. It was one she knew well, and one she was glad to see.

"Not you, too?" Valerie sighed, entering the office.

"You're stuck with me again, Val."

Charlie had been Valerie's partner for the previous 16 months chasing down various fugitives for the FBI. In that time, she had gotten used to his imposing physicality and wit, and his keen hearing.

"Heard me coming, did you?" Valerie asked.

"It's not hard with those heels."

Valerie patted Charlie on the arm and then stepped to the side of his broad-shouldered frame, instinctively reaching out with her hand.

Her boss, Jackson Weller, was sitting behind his desk with a grim look on his face. It made him look at least ten years older than his 52 years on this planet should have. Behind him, the early spring sky glared ominously through a large window.

A sinking feeling fluttered in Valerie's stomach.

The hangover was now gone but was replaced with nerves. She had never seen such an intense look on her boss's face before.

Jackson stood up and shook Valerie's hand.

"Special Agent Law, glad you could make it."

Valerie sat down in the office, surrounded by crammed shelves carrying many leather-bound hardbacks that Jackson liked to lose himself in when he had the time.

An awkward silence grew as Charlie sat in the chair beside her.

Valerie hated tension between colleagues. She had to break it.

"Is this because of what happened in Nashville? Because if it is…" She didn't get to finish her thought.

"You mean," said Jackson Weller, "when you arrested Yulrich Hammond?"

"I profiled his behavior; I could tell he was hiding something about the girl's kidnapper. We didn't have much time. For all I knew she was already dead. I…"

"Don't worry," Jackson said, gently motioning for her to stop. "Technically, you were right. You weren't to know that he was an undercover agent. In fact, it was your ability to deduce from body language alone that he was lying about his identity that's landed you this new position. That and the fact that your profiling of the kidnapper helped us find the girl alive. Upstairs is impressed."

Valerie felt relief course through her veins, but she was wary of an

10

assignment change. She was good at what she did, and she had found a happy niche in her working life.

"What kind of assignment is this?" Charlie asked, always quick to get to the point.

Pulling out a file from his desk drawer, Jackson looked like he had the weight of the world on his shoulders.

"The CPU," Jackson said gravely. "Criminal Psychopathy Unit. It's a new unit we're creating. You two are the first to be recruited. All the details are in here." He tapped the file then slid it across the desk to Valerie. "And there's a good pay bump if you both accept. This is another bite of the apple after the Clawstitch case."

Valerie didn't want to think about the Clawstitch killer case. It was her greatest failure as an agent. If this was another chance to finally progress in her career, she knew it would be her last.

Carefully picking up the file, feeling both elated and nervous at the possibilities, Valerie kept her composure. A level head was desired above all else as an agent.

While her profiling skills had been developed specifically with psychopaths in mind when she was training at the Behavioral Analysis Unit, she rarely got the opportunity to work on such cases, and since her failure to catch the Clawstitch killer, she was thrilled to finally be given a second shot.

Looking at Charlie, she could see he felt the same way. He was like a book to her, but then most people were.

"I know most of your cases have been kidnappers, blackmailers, terrorists, that sort of thing, recently," Weller continued. "But, I have every confidence in you both to apprehend the most violent and depraved fugitives in our country. And so do the higher ups who put you on the team."

"Where will we be stationed?" Charlie asked.

"Here at the Mesmer Building in Quantico," answered Weller. "However, we've yet to assign the necessary office space. This is moving quickly."

"Something forced your hand before the unit was ready?" Valerie asked, one eyebrow raised.

Jackson Weller looked worried, and this vexed Valerie. Not much ruffled her boss, but he seemed overtly tense.

"Your first case has come along quickly, and it's practically on our doorstep in Stafford County, Virginia. In there," Weller said, pointing to the file in Valerie's hand, "you'll find everything you need to get started."

"Who is the perp?" Charlie asked as Valerie scanned the file with her eyes.

She was staring at the cold gaze of a man's mugshot. Something about him immediately put her on edge. Something in his eyes. An emptiness.

A name was printed beneath it.

Blake Harlow.

"You have certain skills that we need," Jackson said, grimly. "And I have to admit you've shown your aptitude to me over the years for tracking people and things down. It's those talents you'll need to rely on the most."

Jackson stood up and then walked over to one of his ornate bookshelves filled with austere hardcovers. He stood in silence for a moment as if pondering the situation.

"Chief, this one seems personal, if you don't mind me saying?" Charlie had a habit of saying what Valerie was thinking.

"Law may be the profiler and you the tracker, Agent Carlson," Jackson replied. "But you have keen senses and insights, too. You're going after one of the most dangerous and depraved individuals it's been my displeasure to meet. Years ago, I was involved in his case. And it's stayed with me. I lost a good partner during the arrest."

Valerie looked at the photo of the perp again.

Blake Harlow was a man who had unnerved one of the FBI's best in Jack Weller. He had sharp features and a darkness beneath his dead eyes that suggested lack of sleep. But the way he stared at the camera unnerved her. He had a slight smirk on his face, and to Valerie it felt like he was sizing up his next meal.

This was underlined by the details of his crimes.

"Blake Harlow escaped from the Culver Institute last night," Weller said, running his hand through his hair and turning to face his two subordinates.

This was a nervous tick Valerie had seen only a couple of times before. It meant Weller anticipated something bad up ahead for all of them.

"I read about the Culver Institute during my training," Valerie offered. "They were controversial at the time."

"Indeed," Jackson said. "They treat these killers with kid gloves for the most part. They think they can cure them."

"You disagree, Chief?" Charlie asked.

"There's no hole in the world deep enough for Blake Harlow after what he did. He showed no mercy to even his own mother years ago. When he was last free, he killed an agent and two others on top of matricide, and we still think he had a hand in several other disappearances... And now he's on the loose." Jackson sat back down at his desk and lowered his voice as if the walls were listening. "He's out there again, and he'll leave death in his wake."

Valerie was multitasking, listening intently while scanning Blake Harlow's file. She was stunned. No profile of him had ever been completed. His victims seemed unrelated, and his personality was so fractured that he could pivot from harmless and confused to murderous and psychotic in the blink of an eye.

Catching someone so unpredictable was going to be a challenge, but one Valerie relished.

"He's the type of individual that your new unit was designed to deal with. A serial killer who doesn't follow the rules. You're not going to learn about someone like this from a textbook.

"Time is of the essence. I've requested that the bodies not be moved until you arrive at the scene. You'll want to look them over. Knowing the perp's past, it won't be a pretty sight, I do warn you.

"The fact this man escaped from a high security ward is an embarrassment, and politically it could get very difficult for those upstairs if he's allowed to kill again. We're being pressured to resolve this quickly. If we don't, the Criminal Psychopathy Unit could be the shortest-lived venture in FBI history."

"We're on it," Valerie said, more determined than ever.

Both agents stood up.

"One more thing," Weller interjected. "And neither of you are going to like it."

"Lay it on us, Chief," said Charlie.

"There is a third man on your team," he said. "A psychiatrist that the higher ups feel can add to the success of your new unit."

"Is that really necessary?" Valeria asked, disheartened by the news that she'd have to hold an academic's hand through their investigation. She had the training. She felt she could handle it.

Jackson stared across his desk at the two FBI agents. "It is with this case. He's an expert on serial killers, though with no experience of tracking fugitives. He has interviewed and studied many of the most dangerous psychopaths in our custody, written some well-respected papers on them."

"Babysitting might slow us down, Chief," Charlie observed. "Can we keep him here at the Mesmer and then consult when we gather evidence?"

Valerie liked that idea. But it was shot down immediately.

"No," Weller answered forcefully. "I know you don't want a stuffy academic hanging around during the chase, but the higher ups have demanded it."

Weller's expression softened to one of sympathy.

"For cases like this, you're going to need all of the help you can get. Prepare yourselves. This killer is capable of anything. He's one of the most brutal murderers I've personally encountered in all my time at the FBI. His previous victims have been butchered like animals… And you're about to come face to face with him. Be careful."

Valeria and Charlie left the office together, but Valerie didn't stop there; she immediately walked at pace down the corridor towards the elevators.

"Are you okay?" asked Charlie, trying to keep up. "I haven't seen you this rattled before."

"We need to get to the Culver Institute immediately," Valeria said quietly as she pushed the button to the elevators. "If what's in this file is even half accurate, there's a bloodbath coming, and we have to stop it."

CHAPTER TWO

"This is going to be horrific," Valerie said as she and Charlie walked along the corridor to Ward 11 of the Culver Institute.

"How bad?" Charlie asked quietly, his polished shoes echoing against the floor.

"The paramedics outside said they'd never seen such a violent attack."

"Agent Law, Agent Carlson, glad you could make it," said a nervous-looking man in glasses and a gray suit at the desk. "My name is Harold Binkley. I'm one of the board members for the Culver Institute. I'm going to oversee your visit.

"We run a fragile operation here... I want to ensure that everything is done with discretion... I still can't believe this has happened."

Charlie and Valerie shook hands with Harold. Valerie tried not to wince at the feel of his clammy hands.

"I know this is a difficult time for you and your colleagues, Mr. Binkley," said Valerie. "But we need to see the bodies immediately. Time is of the essence."

"What will the public think?" the man asked. "We're already in danger of being shut down, then this happens. It won't do at all."

"Are they through here?" Charlie said gravely, pointing at the ward door and clearly annoyed at Binkley's priorities.

Binkley nervously pushed his glasses up his nose.

Valerie sensed from his expression and body language that Binkley was avoiding Charlie's direct question. He didn't want to face the reality of what had happened within the institute's walls.

"I don't mean to say it's not a tragedy," Binkley replied, backtracking somewhat on his apparent iciness. "But we do important work here. Understanding the intersection of criminality and psychopathy could help us cure individuals of their dark, violent impulses. But some don't see it that way. They think we should treat such individuals as fit only for incarceration or worse. What a waste when there's so much to be understood."

Valerie could tell he didn't *really* care about the well-being of his patients. She had trained with many psychologists and psychiatrists as a profiler at the BAU. She remembered quite a few like Harold Binkley: more interested in knowledge than justice. More concerned with insight than the victims of violent crime.

She hid her disgust well, a skill she had learned since a child.

Harold continued his diatribe.

"There are already two senators gunning for us. I mean, have you seen what the papers are saying already?"

"The murders have already been leaked then?" asked Valerie, knowing full well that if the public knew, it would make her job more difficult tracking the perp. There would be more pressure from the politicians. That slid down the food chain to Jackson Weller, and *his* pressure would make the entire situation a powder keg.

If Valerie didn't solve the case quickly, she could and would be easily replaced, despite Jackson's fondness for her.

Binkley nodded and adjusted his black tie as if looking in the mirror. Appearances were clearly important to him.

"Has Dr. Cooper arrived, yet?" Valerie asked.

On their way to the Culver Institute, she had read a little about her new colleague in the file Jackson had given her. But she didn't need to read too much; she was shocked to read that the psychiatrist was very famous in forensic circles. Nonetheless, she still worried about having a psychiatrist second guess her every move or interpretation.

Dr. Cooper would slow her process down.

Binkley shook his head.

"I'm not aware of a Dr. Cooper?"

Charlie and Valerie looked at each other.

A wry smile was shared between them. Valerie knew this was an opportunity to get a head start on the case without the bureaucratic imposition of another expert.

"Let's examine the bodies," Charlie said, walking through the open security door, two security guards standing on either side of it. They nodded, one of them looking at Charlie with a wide stare. Charlie was taller than both, and his broad shoulders could intimidate even those trained to never be intimidated.

Even for Valerie, an experienced profiler and in-the-field investigator for the FBI, what she saw unnerved her.

"When the Chief said it wouldn't be pretty, I guess this is what he meant," Charlie said, studying the scene intently.

Propped up against one of the walls in the corridor was what

16

remained of Dr. Mason Winters.

"Terrible, isn't it? We had to go to the bother of emptying the other cells for fear it might antagonize the other patients." Harold Binkley pulled out a handkerchief and covered his mouth as if frightened of catching something. He looked disgusted rather than aggrieved for the loss of one of his own.

Jackson Weller would never act like that if it was one of us, Valerie thought. Binkley made her skin crawl. She ignored his false posturing and turned to the body on the floor.

Dried blood had dyed Mason Winters's white lab coat a deep crimson red. He had bled out from his throat; his nose and one of his eyes had been heavily disfigured.

His remaining eye stared out, glassy, lifeless, and unable to communicate the terror it had witnessed.

Valerie closed her own eyes for a moment. She didn't want to imagine the mind of a man capable of such horror, never mind immerse herself within it. But that was the job.

"You okay, Valerie?" asked Charlie.

"Yes," she answered.

The smell of blood caught the back of her throat, and yet still her abilities as a profiler began to take over. The only way to service the dead man now was to find the monster responsible.

"Unnecessary facial disfigurement," Charlie said quietly. "Do you think Blake Harlow hated the doctor?"

Valerie thought it through for a moment.

"The killer hates knowledge."

"Knowledge?" Binkley asked, surprised. "As your colleague said, I'd say he hated Dr. Mason Winters himself to do such a thing."

"The wound in the left eye," Valerie continued, her voice steady. "The killer thrust his finger into the eye socket and through the retina and optic nerve. He didn't hate the doctor. He hated the knowledge he possessed. Blake Harlow was trying to destroy the brain, even after expiration."

Binkley cleared his throat.

"The windpipe and vocal cords have been torn and pulled out of the throat," Valerie observed. "This is for a reason. The killer detests those in the psychiatric profession. He is disgusted by their words and theories. Destroy the brain. Destroy the voice."

Binkley rubbed the front of his neck under his chin as if finally feeling some connection to what had befallen Mason Winters.

17

Valerie reached into her inside coat pocket and pulled out a pair of blue latex gloves, which she then pulled on. She hated the feel and look of them. It reminded her of her mother, constantly prodded and touched by medical professionals.

Valerie moved the unbuttoned flap of Mason Winters's white coat. She had spotted something.

In the breast pocket of his shirt, there was a small notebook. Removing it from the pocket, Valerie opened it carefully, noticing bloodied fingerprints all over it. Several pages had been torn from the inside by a bloodied hand.

"Either the killer detested having anything written about him, or Dr. Winters here had jotted down something the killer wants hidden."

"Bravo, Agent Law," a new voice said from behind. The echo of the place carried the same dead reverberation as before, but the voice carried authority with it.

While carrying out her investigation, Valerie had hyper-focused on the body as she always did. She hadn't heard the footsteps of someone else joining them.

She turned to see a professorial looking middle-aged man in a tweed jacket and dark brown bow tie. He was every bit the cliche of an academic, right down to his black rimmed glasses and graying brown hair that needed a comb put through it.

"Very well done," the man said, adjusting his glasses with one hand. "Jackson said you had talent, Agent Law."

"Dr. Cooper?" Charlie asked.

"Yes, indeed," the man answered. "Will Cooper, but our introductions can wait until later. Come with me, would you?" He didn't wait for a reply; instead he moved down the corridor to the last room on the ward.

A chill ran through Valerie. She felt a deep uneasiness toward what she was about to see.

CHAPTER THREE

Valerie felt sideswiped by the arrival of her new teammate to Ward 11.

Another profiler would make her job more difficult, and she felt her heart sink at the thought of future disagreements as they both grappled for the correct interpretation of the killer's behavior

She gave Charlie a knowing glance as they followed Dr. Cooper, their footsteps echoing, then deadened, by the sterile walls.

Charlie shrugged his shoulders in return as if unsure of the situation. Valerie was used to taking the lead. She hadn't even been properly introduced to Dr Cooper, and here he was leading them through Ward 11 to some terrible revelation.

The fact that he had dispensed with usual introductions, made Valerie wonder if he was always going to be that awkward.

"Wait a minute! How did you get in here, Dr. Cooper?" Binkley asked as he hurried alongside.

"Mr. Binkley, is it?" the doctor said as he stopped outside the last room on the ward. "I was given access to the institute by your superiors a couple of hours ago."

Binkley grumbled under his breath.

Valerie peered through the open doorway and saw the carnage. Two security personnel brutally murdered, lying in their own blood and heavily disfigured. The nametags read Larry Makin and Gary Jenkins.

"Agent Law? What do you make of this?" Dr. Cooper asked.

Valerie used tragedies in her work to motivate her to find each criminal she was assigned to. It was all about the families and giving them closure. But even for an agent of her experience, she had never seen anything so violent. She hoped that no one in the victims' families would ask to see the bodies. Not in their mutilated condition.

She looked at the bludgeoned, purpled face of Larry Makin.

"This kill was more personal to the killer," Valerie offered.

"And what makes you say that?" said Dr. Cooper.

"The face has been repeatedly stabbed dozens of times. There was anger here. Unfiltered rage. When we think of people, our brains retrieve an image of them. That image is always what they look like, and that's invariably the face."

"Go on," Dr. Cooper encouraged.

The smell of congealed blood made Valerie want to be sick. It always did. The smell brought back a terrible memory from her childhood involving her mother. But she pushed that memory away quickly as she always did.

Valerie intended to outrun her past no matter what it took.

"The killer wanted to remove Larry Makin's identity," she continued. "He wanted to blot him out from existence. There's no chance of an open casket. No way for a loved one to identify him. This was personal. Time was of the essence to the killer, and yet he took the time to completely violate this man's body. There's a personal relationship here. A history. I'd suggest the possibility that Larry Makin had been less than kind to Blake Harlow during his incarceration here."

"That makes sense," Charlie offered. "The other guard's wounds aren't as horrific."

"Yes," Valerie answered before the psychiatrist could. "Gary Jenkins's eyes have been stabbed out. The killer didn't like the way he looked at him, but the kill was quick. Larry here, on the other hand, was punished."

"Excellent, Agent Law," said Dr. Cooper. "You're everything Jackson Weller said you'd be."

"Do you have everything you need, Val?" Charlie asked. "I'd like to liaise with local law enforcement as soon as possible to see if there have been any sightings."

"Ah, can't wait to get your man, Agent Carlson? Can't say the chasing part is my forte," Doctor Cooper said, looking at the bodies somberly before turning to Valerie. "You know, I was sitting in Dr Winters's office earlier, reading through his notes and case files. Such a shame, I think he had the makings of an excellent profiler if he'd decided to go in that direction."

"Quite," Binkley sniped.

"Tell me, Agent Law, have you had a chance to look over the patient's file yet?" Dr. Cooper stood there looking on quizzically, one eyebrow raised and his stare a hopeful one.

The doctor wasn't what Valerie had imagined.

When she had been told that a psychiatrist was going to accompany her and Charlie on the case, she had already conceived of several ways

20

they could tie him up in administrative work while she and her partner got down to the nitty gritty of catching the escaped patient.

There was something both young and old about Dr. Cooper, something wise and brash. If he was as brilliant as his reputation, he might prove useful yet.

"From what I can see, he's a classic psychopath with narcissistic tendencies, but… There's something deeper going on here," Valerie said. "There's a rage. The way he's mutilated the victims. I can't put my finger on it, but I'd say there's a history that might lead us to him.

"Anger like that is usually born out of insecurity and trauma. But there's not much in the FBI's files other than his rap sheet. He'd rarely make sense during interviews. I guess that's what poor Doctor Winters was supposed to be tending to."

"And what about you, Agent Carlson? Any insight?" the psychiatrist asked.

Charlie laughed.

"I leave the insight to Valerie here. My talent is…"

"Catching people who do not want to get caught, eh?" Will smiled.

Charlie nodded.

"I suppose you could put it that way."

"But not quite just the brawn to Agent Law's brain? Surely more?"

"Agent Carlson is being modest," said Valerie. "He likes people to underestimate him so he can over-perform."

Charlie grinned.

"He's given me insights on cases that I wouldn't have found on my own. Many times, in fact."

"That's reassuring," Will said, pulling out a notepad from his inside pocket. "Now, I've jotted down some notes from Dr. Winters's own files. It seems that our patient *did* divulge one interesting piece of information to him during previous meetings."

"I think I should really look those over first," Binkley said, having stayed silent for longer than he seemed comfortable.

"And I think," Will said not looking up from his notebook, "that you should be more worried about Dr Winters's professional opinion than being nosy."

Binkley's gaze narrowed.

"And what is that supposed to mean?"

Will finally looked up from his notes. Valerie noticed a change in his expression. He was vexed by something.

"The dead cannot speak for themselves," Will said, sharply. "So allow us to be their representatives. Dr. Winters made no less than three complaints about security procedures specifically involving the patient, did he not?"

"Well… I…," Binkley's face flushed red.

"It appears that the good doctor was reprimanded by you directly for, and I quote, 'causing trouble.' Perhaps in the future, you should listen to the experts who are working with your patients and follow through on their recommendations."

"I don't have to…"

"Stand for this?" Will finished Binkley's sentence. "No, you don't. You can be on your way if you wish, but remember, you have the luxury to walk out of here, the departed Dr. Mason Winters does not. He will be carried out in a body bag."

"That is an outrageous thing to say!" But no one took the bite. Binkley just slithered off up the corridor, stopping momentarily to look at Doctor Winters's body before exiting Ward 11.

Valerie was surprised by Doctor Cooper's confrontational turn. She liked it.

"So, did you find any leads in Doctor Winters's notes, Doctor Cooper?" Valerie asked.

"Yes," he replied, excitedly. "The only time the patient spoke of anything personal was during a conversation several nights ago. He told Dr. Winters that he felt there was a 'synchronicity' to him being at the Culver Institute."

"Synchronicity?" Charlie mused. "Like Carl Jung?"

Will looked surprised.

"Yes, Agent Carlson. Exactly! That's very impressive."

"I have to read up on things so I can occasionally tell Valerie when she's wrong."

Valerie gave a sarcastic roll of her eyes.

"Well," continued Will. "Synchronicity is indeed a concept from Carl Jung, about coincidences. He believed that some coincidences were so unlikely and profound, that they were not sheer accidents.

"The patient believed that coming to the Culver Institute itself was synchronicity."

"Had he been here before?" Charlie asked.

"Not that I could see from his file," Valerie said. "But it is a fascinating coincidence how close the institute is to where he used to live."

"Yes, exactly," Doctor Cooper said. "And I wonder, given the fact that he mentioned a strange coincidence in these notes, that Blake Harlow won't be motivated to visit some of these old haunts."

"The orphanage!" suggested Valerie. "That was in his file, and it does seem to be a pretty meaningful coincidence… Oh God…"

"What?" asked Charlie.

"Charlie, radio local law enforcement to head on over to Bristlewood Orphanage. We'll meet them there!" Valerie said, turning and rushing towards the ward door.

"The orphanage is still in use," she continued, hurriedly. "Blake Harlow's profile shows he has no specific victim type. He could target anyone. There's no telling what he might do to the kids there."

CHAPTER FOUR

Valerie felt the car lurch on the wet highway road as Charlie jerked the wheel, weaving in and out of traffic.

The streets of Stafford County blurred in the distance beneath the graying sky, the early spring weather more biting than usual.

Looking in the rearview mirror, she could see Doctor Cooper looking nervous, patting his brow with a white handkerchief.

"Don't you have a siren or lights to clear the road?" he asked, his voice slightly panicked.

"That's just in movies, Doctor Cooper," Charlie said, never taking his eyes off the road. "Sirens are for emergency services. You know, police, ambulances, that sort of thing."

Charlie gripped the wheel tightly as the car followed a tight corner.

The doctor let out an audible gasp. "But isn't this an emergency?"

"You're not used to field work, are you Doctor Cooper?" Valerie asked.

"Please," he replied, wiping his brow again. "Call me Will. If we're going to work together, we should dispense with formalities... And yes, I'm not used to this sort of thing."

Valerie looked to the road ahead, the rain cascading off it, making the world seem more uncertain than it needed to be. She just hoped they'd make it to the orphanage in time before Blake Harlow could carry out another twisted attack.

"I guess we'll all have to lean on each other, then, Will. We'll help you with field work; you help us with getting into the killer's mind. Deal?"

"That's an idea," Will said, checking his seat belt.

"Do you really think he'd kill at the orphanage?" Charlie asked, the sound of rain battering the car roof above.

Valerie looked down at the file in her lap. She opened it and looked at that cold stare again in the mugshot. Blake Harlow gazed back.

Turning the page, she read the pathologist's summary of the killer's first ever known victim.

Crushed... Bludgeoned... Disemboweled...

The crime scene photos soon followed, far worse than any description.

"Valerie?" Charlie said, reminding her that he'd asked a question.

"Yeah, I think he could kill at the orphanage," she answered in a somber voice. "You saw the bodies at the Culver Institute. Anyone with that amount of rage inside is capable of anything. We'll need to be on our toes."

"I agree," Will said from the backseat, the rain flooding down the window to the rear of him. "From Doctor Winters's notes, Blake Harlow possesses intelligence, a fragmentary personality, and sadistic tendencies. A potent combination for any killer."

"Undoubtedly faced brutal abuse as a child, I'd say," Valerie observed.

"Don't be so sure," answered Will.

"But most violent killers are made, Doctor."

"Most, yes. But some are born," Will's voice tailed off.

"Sounds like you've had some experience of that," Charlie interjected.

The road ahead seemed to go on for infinity, swallowed up on the horizon by the unrelenting rain.

Will cleared his throat as if composing himself.

"I've treated many psychopaths, but this one is unique. If Blake Harlow has gone to the orphanage," he said, "he's at least more predictable than I initially expected. That will give us an advantage in catching him."

Valerie's phone pinged with a message just as she was listening to Will's words.

She looked down at her phone as the car headed off the main highway and onto a narrow country road, splashing through several puddles.

Her blood ran cold at the name of the sender.

It simply read: *Sister*.

For a moment, Valerie was transfixed by the name, staring at it as the world around her became a blur. She hadn't spoken to her sister in two years, and four before that.

Valerie saw a flash of hurt in her mind, all brought into focus from the text message. It was a memory: an image of her mother and sister. Their mother was standing over both her girls waving a knife and screaming.

Closing her eyes, Valerie tried to wash the memory away.

25

She had a little trick she'd learned from one of several failed therapy groups she attended when she was younger. When dealing with post-traumatic stress, powerful and disturbing images of past events often become intrusive thoughts. The only thing you can do to rid yourself of these intrusions is to have an anchor, an anchor in the storm, as it had been put to her.

Valerie's anchor was another memory.

A memory of her Uncle Jason. It was on a clear June day. Valerie was nine years old. She was watching a sea of green apples swaying on the branches of a large tree. Suddenly, Uncle Jason picked her up so she could reach one. Her uncle had a water bottle with him and poured it over the apple, cleaning it. Then, he handed it back to his young niece with a kind smile.

This was a good memory. A moment of kindness among the dark clouds of her childhood. It was precious. And it helped.

I can't go back to there, she thought, deleting the message without reading it.

"You okay, Val?"

"Uh... Yes, I'm fine, Charlie," she replied. "Not long to go. The orphanage should be at the end of this road. I just hope we're in time."

"Are you sure?" Will asked. "I don't mean to pry, but that message seemed to upset you. Please tell me nothing has happened at the orphanage?"

"No... It's nothing. Thank you."

Valerie turned and looked to the back seat. Will was staring at her. He wore on his face a penetrating look that Valerie felt strike at her deepest anxieties.

He knows, she thought to herself. *He knows there's something wrong with me.*

"It's nothing, Will. Honestly." The lie came easily out of Valerie's mouth. But it always did when she needed to cover up the past.

Another text arrived.

It was from her sister again.

What if she's hurt? Valerie thought.

Unable to ignore it this time, she opened the message, read it, and then put her phone away.

Valerie had retreated into her own thoughts. The message read: "We need to talk about Mom."

There was no way she could get into it with her sister.

Not there.

Not in the car with her colleagues on the trail of a deadly killer. But Valerie knew deep down that it would have to be answered eventually, one way or another. But any time she had spoken with her sister about their mother, it had pulled at her well-being like a loose thread, unraveling until she was exposed to the world.

Vulnerability was not an option in Valerie's world. Not now. Not ever.

"Looks like we're here," Charlie said as two large iron gates came into view and then opened, allowing the car onto a large estate.

Passing through a copse of trees and then over a small, humped back bridge, the trees opened up like a wound to reveal a large, dominant country house made of red sandstone.

"The orphanage," Will said.

"God dammit, I don't see a patrol car," observed Charlie. "How did we get here first?"

He checked his gun on his shoulder holster.

Valerie did the same.

"I can't see any forced entry from here," Charlie said. "But we'll need to get closer."

"Maybe you should stay in the car, Will?" suggested Valerie.

"No," Will said, obviously putting on a brave face. "I'll come with you. I might still be of some help."

"Let's get in there and see what we can find." Valerie said. "But, Will, if things go bad, duck and cover, okay?"

Will nodded.

They left the car and walked slowly towards the building. The rain fell around them, covering their footsteps in white noise. Valerie thought for a moment that if Blake Harlow were already there, they wouldn't hear him coming.

A monster in the rain. Death and madness in his eyes.

Valerie watched the curtained windows of Bristlewood Orphanage peering down at her like a hundred accusing eyes.

Just as they reached the foot of the steps out front, the large oak doors above them opened.

Valerie drew her gun.

CHAPTER FIVE

Valerie, unwilling to wait another second, slammed the side of her fist onto the oak door of the office three times. The knocks echoed out to far off places inside Bristlewood Orphanage, loud enough to wake the dead if it had been night.

The trembling receptionist who had greeted them at the door of the orphanage had told them Miss Armstrong didn't like to have her schedule ruffled.

Valerie didn't care.

She knew they were running out of time before Blake Harlow killed again.

"This place gives me the creeps," Charlie said.

"It does feel antiquated," Will added.

The corridor was harshly lit by fluorescent lighting, jarring with the Victorian era wooden paneling and decor. The air moved with an unsettling chill through it, and Valerie felt that the atmosphere was far from welcoming for visitors, let alone orphaned children.

She banged the door again, more forceful this time.

The golden name plate reading "Miss Armstrong" rattled on its fittings to the oak door.

But the door didn't open.

"Feels like we're being made to wait like one of their kids," Charlie observed.

"Just a few more minutes," a thin voice said from beyond the door. "I have some important paperwork that *must* be attended to."

Valerie moved her hand towards the brass handle in front of her. Its deep sheen contorted the shadows of the corridor, shaping the world into a mirrored nightmare.

"Perhaps we should show some tact," Will suggested. "We don't want to make any enemies here. We may need access to their records to understand Blake Harlow in greater depth."

Valerie didn't listen. She knew when someone was playing games.

She grabbed the brass handle, the coldness of it as uncomfortable as the air, and opened the door, stepping inside to an office that was shrouded in deep red wooden paneling and aging leather-bound books.

An elderly lady in a pristine gray suit sat behind a mahogany desk.

Her hair was white with a few sporadic wisps of gray, and it was pulled back so tightly in a bun that the veins in her forehead were like spider legs.

She glared at Valerie and her two colleagues as they entered uninvited.

"Just a minute!" she said, rising to her feet sharply. "I told you to wait."

"And I told your receptionist that there's a killer on the loose," replied Valerie. "For your own safety and the safety of the children here at the orphanage, we need to talk. Now."

"I received your message. We have our own security personnel here, I'm quite sure…"

"We're here about Blake Harlow, Miss Armstrong," Will interjected.

If it were possible, Miss Armstrong's face grew paler. She sat down slowly.

"A very troubled boy," she said quietly.

"More than troubled," added Charlie. "Are you aware of his crimes?"

Miss Armstrong nodded.

"He's escaped from a maximum-security psychiatric ward," said Valerie. "And we suspect he may try to come here, as the orphanage has significance for him."

"This is intolerable."

"Forgive our intrusion, Miss Armstrong," said Will. "But as you can see, this is a grave situation, and we would be grateful for your help as Bristlewood Orphanage's head mistress. If there's anything in your records…"

As Will spoke, Valerie considered Miss Armstrong.

Her desk was large and sprawling, her seat slightly raised, making her look like a queen of old, and on the east wall between two bookcases was a painting of the woman herself.

The artist had been overly kind in toning down the head mistress's cold demeanor and accusatory stare.

On the opposite wall were a few photographs of Miss Armstrong meeting important figures: mayors, senators, even a few celebrities. All wide grins and white teeth.

Valerie observed that there wasn't one picture of the children from the orphanage on the walls, not even a group photo with Miss Armstrong and her staff.

She cares more about her status than the children, Valerie thought to herself. And when someone cared only about themselves, Valerie knew to use this to her advantage.

"Perhaps we got off on the wrong foot… I take it you were already working at Bristlewood when Blake Harlow was here as a child?" asked Valerie.

"Yes. I was head mistress back then, but new to the role. It was an exciting time for me, but not without challenge."

Miss Armstrong's answer confirmed Valerie's suspicions about her priorities.

Rather than giving information about Blake Harlow or asking about the safety of the children at the orphanage, she had brought the focus back around to herself as the topic of conversation.

Valerie decided to use this to delve deeper.

"It must take its toll trying to guide children into better ways of behaving."

"Indeed!" Miss Armstrong's eyes lit up, seemingly fueled by the compliment and understanding shown by Valerie. "Teaching is a terrible burden, but one we must rise to if the children are to thrive later."

"I envy those with the patience." Valerie didn't want to lay it on too thick, but she knew what she was doing. Soon, she'd turn the screw.

"Thank you, one does require patience and self-discipline. Too many bleeding hearts these days in the profession, I have to say. They don't realize that it's for the good of the children that we stay strong."

"I see you've garnered a lot of prestige," Valerie said, pointing to the walls filled with photographs and awards.

"Yes, quite," Miss Armstrong replied. "But this is not a motivation for doing important work that contributes to wider society, of course."

Miss Armstrong momentarily showed signs of modesty and discomfort at being so praised. Valerie didn't buy it for a second.

With every exchange, Miss Armstrong was becoming more open to Valerie's approach. Little did she know that each response, each small movement of her eyes whenever she broke and then re-engaged eye-contact, each and every movement of her hands suggesting a closed, defensive feeling - these were being noted mentally by Valerie.

A profile of Miss Armstrong was building quickly. And it was not a flattering one. *Narcissistic, glory hunting, lack of empathetic emotion*:

30

These were not ideal traits for a teacher.

As the Head Mistress kept a weathered smile on her face, Valerie felt it was time to change tact and take her by surprise.

"And what happens when things go wrong, Miss Armstrong?" she asked.

"Wrong?"

"Yes, wrong," repeated Valerie. "What happens when someone like Blake Harlow turns out bad. How does that happen?"

Miss Armstrong seemed flustered by the mention of that name.

"Well," she said, clearing her throat. "Some children are broken when they arrive and cannot be fixed."

"It sounds like you think they're toys to be tinkered with," Charlie interjected.

A scowl momentarily flickered across Miss Armstrong's face, pointed directly at Charlie. But if the mask had slipped, it was quickly reattached.

Valerie was thankful for Charlie. He always had a way of perceptively stripping someone of their psychological armor and summing up their maladaptive traits concisely.

"What exactly is it that you want from me?" Miss Armstrong asked.

"Miss Armstrong," Valerie took a small black notepad and pen out of her inside pocket to jot down her observations. "Blake Harlow has killed again. He has escaped. And we believe he might come back here, if he isn't here already. We need to secure the orphanage immediately. And the more you can tell us about Blake's past here, the better chance we have of predicting his behavior and catching him before he kills again. It could be you, one of your staff, or even the kids."

"Dear God." Miss Armstrong rubbed her veined forehead with her hand. She seemed anxious, but then looked up as though her frozen composure had returned.

"I'm sure our security guards will be able to deal with him if he shows his face."

"That's what they thought at the Culver Institute where he was being kept," Charlie offered. "Several security guards and a psychiatrist were murdered and mutilated there. You can assume they were much better trained than the guards you have here."

Valerie noticed a brief look on Miss Armstrong's face. It was as if she was more aggravated than afraid. And that was a strange reaction to the danger Blake Harlow presented.

"Local law enforcement will provide a presence in the building

31

until we can be sure everyone here is safe," Valerie said bluntly.

"Absolutely not!" Miss Armstrong sniped. "I've already told the officers outside waiting in their patrol cars that their presence here is an obscenity."

"If Blake Harlow gets into this building," Valeria stated, coolly. "If he does... There's every chance more blood will be spilled. It could even be yours."

"I will not be threatened by the FBI" the old lady said. "We have a set routine here, something that must be maintained for the children to learn correct behaviors.

"The children are severely affected by any alterations to this routine. The very presence of police officers and their guns, well, that's the sort of thing that fuels wagging tongues and rumors about the orphanage's hypothetical failings, not to mention affecting how the children can learn and play.

"I won't have our children or anyone else insinuate that Bristlewood Orphanage is anything but a sanctuary."

"But surely...," Charlie said before being cut off.

"Surely nothing," Miss Armstrong interrupted. "It is my duty as head mistress to navigate difficult times and ensure our children are taken care of as normal."

"Listen, Miss Armstrong," Charlie said, biting back. "If we choose to cram this place with agents, hell, even have one sitting at your desk for company, then we'll do it."

"I won't stand for this!"

Valerie found it increasingly strange that the head mistress wasn't concerned for the safety of the staff or children. Something about her approach to their questions seemed off.

She's hiding something, Valerie thought.

"Perhaps, if I may," Will said, having been silent and watchful for some time, "a compromise of having some unmarked patrol cars sitting on the grounds instead of those with overtly flashing lights, would be better? That way, no one need know there is a police presence, and the children won't be disturbed?"

Silence fell across the room for a moment as Miss Armstrong considered Will.

Valerie observed a flicker in her eyes. That flicker conveyed discomfort, as if the head mistress was getting ready for another battle.

An idea began to formulate in Valerie's mind. There was something going on at Bristlewood. Something strange. She could read it in every line of Miss Armstrong's disgruntled face. Perhaps making her feel a little more at ease would open up an opportunity to find out more.

"Will's idea is a good one," Valerie said. "And it's the best you're going to get."

"I will accept this," Miss Armstrong soon said, begrudgingly. "But I do not want them inside the building unless absolutely necessary. The lives of the children must not be disturbed. They are, after all, fragile."

"It's at least something," Charlie said turning to Valerie, in a persuasive tone.

"Okay," Valeria said reluctantly. "Charlie, contact local law enforcement, see if we can get some plain clothes units on the grounds. But I don't want anyone coming in or out of Bristlewood without us knowing about it."

"I'll get on it," Charlie said, standing up and walking to the door.

Valerie gave the head mistress a knowing glance.

"And do a sweep of the building, Charlie. Just to make sure Blake didn't get here before us."

"I said I didn't want any police skulking around!" Miss Armstrong said, agitated.

"We're not police," said Valerie with authority. "In any case, if we had good cause to believe Blake Harlow were here and ready to kill again, Charlie could search the premises as a Federal Agent. Or...," Valerie smiled. "I could speak with Social Services and get a court order to temporarily shut this place down as unsafe? Which would you prefer?"

"Very well," Miss Armstrong scowled.

Charlie smiled and left the room, closing the door behind him. Valerie could hear his footsteps echoing in the cold corridor beyond.

"If you'll excuse me, I have some things I..."

"We're not done, Miss Armstrong," said Valerie. "We need to know more about Blake Harlow, his past, and why he would want to come back here."

"I have no idea why."

"Was he mistreated here?"

Miss Armstrong drew Valerie another harsh, accusatory look.

"*No one* at Bristlewood is mistreated, young lady. Are we strict? Absolutely! We have to be. Many of the children here come from difficult backgrounds and have acquired antisocial behaviors of which we must rid them."

"And how do you do that, Miss Armstrong?" Valeria asked.

"Discipline. Routine. Ethics. All of these are important."

"Was Blake Harlow subjected to the same methods?" Valerie's pen hovered over the white paper of her notepad, waiting for an answer.

"Times have changed," Miss Armstrong frowned. "Perhaps our methods have… Mellowed with those times."

"So, do you think Blake could have a score to settle with someone who was *too* firm?" Will interjected, pushing his glasses back up the bridge of his nose.

"We have had hundreds, if not thousands of children pass through our halls since Blake Harlow. None of them are serial killers that I know of."

"Except Blake," Valeria corrected.

"Except Blake. Yes. So, I infer from that, that whatever damage or evil resides in that man, it was there before he came here."

"You blame the parents then?" Will pushed.

"The apple rarely falls far from the tree," Miss Armstrong said, her words ice cold. "I'm surprised his brother turned out as well as he did in the end."

"As he did?" Valerie asked, curious. "Is he still in touch with the orphanage?"

"Why, yes," answered Miss Armstrong. "He has come by and given some talks now and then. I'm very proud of the work we did with him. A fine example of Bristlewood at work."

"He's not here today, is he?" Will asked, his voice sounding worried.

"No," the head mistress answered. "I believe he was moving house the last time he spoke with my secretary."

"Far away, I hope?" Will asked.

"Oh dear, no," the old lady said.

It was clear to Valerie that the worry now apparent in Miss Armstrong's voice was a little too put on.

"I believe he moved back to the local area, Elm Lane in fact." The old head mistress seemed to lose control of her harsh expression momentarily. A slight grin came and went from the corners of her mouth.

She thinks she can get out us out of here, and quick, Valerie thought.

"I would have thought the FBI would have kept an eye on him, if they thought he was in danger," the old head mistress said in a wry tone.

"No one expected the man to escape from where he was," Valerie said, trying to defend their situation. "Can you give me the address of the brother, and the last known address of the couple who adopted them?"

"Your records really are lacking, my dear," Miss Armstrong said, grinning. "Of course, Bristlewood Orphanage to the rescue as per usual. I'll have my secretary give you the details. Now, may *I* be excused?"

Valerie nodded.

"Thank you for your assistance, Miss Armstrong," Will said.

"Oh, one more thing, Miss Armstrong," Valerie smiled.

Miss Armstrong looked as cold as ever.

"I'll put in a call with the orphanage's board of directors," Valerie said standing up.

"Why!" Miss Armstrong's mask was finally slipping for good.

Valerie pointed to one of the certificates on the wall behind the sneering woman.

"That certificate of inspection is five years old. I'll help get the ball moving with a new inspection for you, just to make sure everything is as it should be here, and the kids are getting the best possible care."

"How dare you!" Miss Armstrong said, slamming her fist onto the desk and standing up.

Despite the woman's advancing years, Valerie found it easy to imagine how frightening the head mistress was to the children in her care.

"Have a nice day, Miss Armstrong," Valerie said, turning and opening the door.

Will had a shocked smile on his face as he followed.

They exited the office into the corridor. Both looked at each other.

"Well," said Will with a whisper. "I see you don't mind ruffling feathers."

"In field work, Will, you sometimes have to. When people are stressed, they often show their intentions, even if they want to keep them hidden. Miss Armstrong was here when Blake Harlow was a child, and I suspect she had a hand in creating the monster we're now chasing. The more we know about his feelings and experiences, the better chance we have of predicting his next move."

Valerie looked around at the cold corridor as they walked away from the office.

"There's something going on here," she said quietly, worried that her words would echo back to the head mistress.

35

"I quite agree," said Will. "Miss Armstrong was overly defensive and far too keen to have us gone. Her body language too, crossing her arms, shielding herself as it were. But what could she be hiding?"

Valerie's cellphone burst into life playing Run Baby Run.

Will smiled.

"Charlie?" Valerie said, answering it.

"I think Blake Harlow is already inside the orphanage," Charlie said over the phone in a hushed tone.

Valerie's blood grew cold, she drew her gun.

"Where are you in the building? Have you called for backup?"

But there was no reply. The phone had gone dead.

CHAPTER SIX

"Will, get back to the car and lock the doors," Valerie said, checking the clip in her gun. As she slid it out and in again, the click echoed against Bristlewood's cold innards.

"I want to help," Will offered.

Valerie appreciated that. But it was too dangerous.

"There should be two officers posted outside," Valerie said, gently. "Tell them to round up the kids as quietly as possible. And you, Will, stay in the car and lock the doors."

"But…," Will didn't have a chance to finish that sentence.

Valerie had already turned a corner, moving further into the embrace of Bristlewood's shadowy hallways.

"Charlie, you there?" she said into her radio as she walked, gun drawn.

There was no reply. And it was the fifth time she'd tried.

Her heart sank at the thought of Charlie being the latest victim in Blake Harlow's killing spree. He was her partner. They always looked out for each other. But he was also her friend. One of the best.

As she moved around another corner as quietly as possible, her thoughts turned to two separate occasions when Charlie had come to her rescue during a case. In one instance, Valerie had been under fire and if he hadn't turned up, she'd be dead.

Valerie moved down another long corridor. She had no knowledge of Bristlewood's layout, but she had seen the rectangular shape of the building on approach. The corridors were laid out in a sort of lattice, and as she moved towards the rear of the building, any sounds of children being taught or interacted with faded.

Valerie was shocked at how the building was in disrepair the further back she went.

Just as she was about to give up and head upstairs to the next floor, she saw something on the floor next to a busted wooden panel.

The panel looked as if something had been smashed into it, and there was the unmistakable glint of blood dripping from the crack.

Valerie moved forward towards the blood, keeping her eyes and gun trained on a nearby doorway. She imagined the ominous figure of Blake Harlow emerging from it, eyes wide and lusting after another kill.

Looking at the blood, it was fresh. Whatever had happened there, happened within minutes of her getting there. She knew she was on the right track. Her stomach churned as she thought about what she might find by looking further.

Another few footsteps and Valerie was around a corner, staring at a forgotten piece of Bristlewood's history. With each twist and turn, the upkeep of that part of the building was almost non-existent.

Light fittings drooped from the ceiling, swaying on old wiring, the sound of a leak somewhere nearby drip, drip, dripped, and there was… a gun.

Valerie's heart raced. On the ground was a gun. Not just *a* gun, but Charlie's Glock 9. She knew it immediately.

Charlie would never abandon his gun. He was ex-Army. Trained to the hilt. And as smart as they came. If he was separated from his weapon, it was because something terrible had happened to him. Valerie was deeply worried for her partner.

Valerie was suddenly conscious of her shoes clicking against the hard flooring. If someone was near, they'd hear.

She slipped off her shoes and hid them inside the doorway of an empty room, then she continued down the hallway, her footsteps now hidden from prying ears.

As she turned into another long corridor, Valerie noticed that the light fitting halfway along wasn't working. That section was bathed in shadow. She took one step towards it, and then quickly hid in the nearest doorway.

Someone was standing in the shadows. Tall, menacing, it could only be one person to Valerie. She had just seen the sinister outline of Blake Harlow, prowling the corridors of the orphanage where he was once partly raised.

Valerie peeked out from the doorway back along the corridor. There was no sign of the man.

Why didn't I shout freeze? she thought.

She had hesitated. That wasn't like her. *Too much on my mind.*

Just as she thought the man had disappeared around a corner, she saw him reappear from a darkened doorway. He was carrying something in his hand. It was rope; Valerie could see it dangling and swaying in his grip.

Raising her gun silently, she pointed it at the man, getting ready to stop him. But instead, something stayed her hand and her voice.

Where's Charlie? What's he done with him?

Going by the blood she'd found on the floor, Valerie reasoned that Charlie was injured. And that Blake Harlow had stashed his body somewhere. She was hopeful that the rope was there to tie him up, meaning her partner was still alive. But where? If he was bleeding out, she'd need to find him quickly. Given the labyrinthine nature of the orphanage, Charlie could have been lying anywhere, and there was no guarantee the killer would reveal the location.

Valerie then made a call against procedure.

She'd follow Harlow to Charlie. Then she would make the arrest. Not before.

As soon as the man moved further down the corridor and around a bend, Valerie moved quickly, silently.

Reaching the corner, she peered round it. Harlow was moving with purpose.

Valerie kept her distance, but kept on him. Three more twists and turns, and finally, he moved into a room. A click sounded and a yellow incandescent glow came through the doorway.

Valerie knew now that Harlow would see her coming. The advantage the shadows gave her had been removed.

Then, she listened.

She could hear something.

It was a low murmur. Through the mortar and wood of that old building, it sounded like a whisper that raised up and lowered.

Her senses were keen, the uninitiated might have thought these sounds were the wind making its way through unseen cracks from outside, but not Valerie. She knew the subtleties of the human voice. And she knew when it was intent on harm.

The voice was coming from inside the room.

No, not one voice, but two.

Valerie's heart sank. The second voice was that of a child. A young girl who sounded afraid.

"Please, no," the girl said, her voice trembling.

Those frightened words cut Valerie deeply. She remembered the trauma of fearing her own mother. She and her sister. An adult using their stature and voice to demean and frighten.

Valerie wasn't going to wait for back up. She had to stop this.

"It'll be over in a moment," the man's voice said from inside the room.

The child cried.

Valerie moved with purpose.

She rushed forward into the room.

Beneath the glare of a solitary light bulb was a young girl with brown hair and her hands tied with rope. Her eyes were filled with tears and fear in equal measure.

Blake, dressed in a shirt and black trousers, stood with his back to Valerie. He loomed over the young girl, one fist clenched in front of her face as she trembled.

Turning his head slightly, he responded to Valerie's footsteps.

"Get out!" the man yelled, reaching over to pick up a piece of metal piping on an old school desk next to him. He turned and threw it.

His body had obscured the move, and this gave Valerie only a fraction of a second to react. The pipe caught Valerie on the side of the head as she let off a shot. A flash spread across her vision momentarily as the shock of the impact dazed her.

The gun was then wrenched from her grip.

But Valerie moved forward relentless, she lurched with her body, ramming her shoulder into the man's gut.

"Run!" she screamed to the girl.

And the girl did, through the door yelling for help. The voice was quickly answered by movement in the building.

The man now reasserted himself and used his strength against Valerie. As he wrapped his arm around her neck, a set of footsteps rushed outside along the corridor towards the room.

Charlie, blood dripping down his forehead, came powering through the doorway.

Valerie elbowed the man in the stomach, breaking from his grip, but he threw her to the floor, and she fell, dazed.

The man was at least Charlie's size, and he knew how to fight, swinging his knee into Charlie's side and tossing him to the side, using Charlie's momentum against him.

Charlie fell into an old desk, the wooden corner jabbing deep into his ribs. He gasped as the wind was knocked from him.

The man picked up the piece of metal piping on the floor and stepped over Charlie. He loomed large, his face cast in shadow with the yellow bulb behind him.

Most would have been frightened. Charlie gasped for air.

Reaching out with his leg, he gave a powerful kick to the man's knee.

Something cracked inside.

The man let out a horrid cry like a wounded animal. He fell forward, losing his footing, swinging down with the metal pipe in his hand.

Charlie moved his head to the side, the pipe splintering the wooden floor next to his ear.

They struggled, and the man dropped the pipe to wrap his hands around Charlie's throat. That was a mistake; it left him open, and Charlie's years of martial arts training took over.

He allowed the choke and thrust upward, catching the man's jaw with tremendous force. Valerie then rose up behind Harlow, pipe in hand, and cracked him across the back of the head. He went limp and fell, dazed over an old chair.

Getting to his feet, exhausted, Charlie peered down at the unconscious man.

"Dammit," Valerie said under her breath as she rubbed her side. "It's not him!"

Charlie didn't reply. He was too tired.

"You okay?" Valerie asked, concerned for her partner.

"I guess," Charlie answered, holding his head.

"I'm glad you're alive," Valerie said, breathing heavily.

"Nice to know you care, Val," Charlie smiled. Then the smile faded, and he pointed to the man on the ground.

"This isn't Blake Harlow," Valerie glared at the man under the light, unable to hide the disappointment.

"Then who is he?" asked Charlie.

"He was in here with a young girl," Valerie said as she leaned down and put the still unconscious man's hands in cuffs. "Let's ask her."

Valerie looked around the disused room with distrust in her eyes. "And find out what the hell is happening in this place."

CHAPTER SEVEN

If the man hadn't been in handcuffs, Valerie was certain he would have delighted in throttling the life from her.

"Keep steady," she said, her hand gripping his arm. "I don't want to have to hurt you."

The man said nothing as Valerie and Charlie led him out, exiting the front of the orphanage. Occasionally, the man would try to pull away from their grip. But the two FBI agents held tight.

Outside of Bristlewood Orphanage beneath a darkening sky, blue and red lights flashed from several parked police cars and an ambulance. They had been called while the orphanage nurse patched up the cut on Charlie's head.

"He's under arrest for assault with a deadly weapon," Charlie said as two cops met them. "And for abusing a child."

The officers took the prisoner away, putting him in the back of a patrol car. He stared at the two agents through the glass.

Valerie ignored one gaze for another. She looked up at one of the countless windows of Bristlewood Orphanage. Miss Armstrong stood between two lavish curtains, peering down with a vengeful scowl.

"I bet she doesn't like this," Charlie said to Valerie as a medic came over to check his head wound.

"Good," Valerie said. "There's something rotten about this place, and I can't help but think it had a hand in making Blake Harlow the violent psychopath he is." She turned to Charlie, "Are you feeling okay?"

"I'll live," Charlie replied. "I started tracking this guy through the building, certain it was Harlow. He caught on and rushed around a corner. I didn't know the layout of the building the way he did. In seconds, he was able to move through a room with another exit, double back and then attack me from behind. I lost my gun in the fight and must have taken a wrong turn trying to chase him after that. This place is like a labyrinth inside."

"It's okay, Charlie," Valerie offered. "I won't put anything in the report about you losing your weapon." Valerie knew how much that was frowned upon. Losing your weapon so that a criminal or a bystander could pick it up was something that could have been used against him later.

It would be an omission on Valerie's part, rather than a lie. Charlie was the best agent she'd ever worked with, and she'd always protect him the way he protected her.

Charlie sighed. "I feel I got sloppy. I was so eager to catch this guy."

"Maybe we all need to be careful about rushing in."

Charlie nodded.

Valerie saw the tired look in Charlie's eyes. He would need to rest. They all would. But with a violent killer on the loose, there was no time for that.

She then noticed that Will was outside talking with a young girl wrapped in a blanket at the back of an ambulance.

"Is that the girl you saved, Val?" Charlie asked.

"Yes," answered Valerie.

The girl looked so fragile to Valerie. She remembered a similar night when she was a child. The howling red and blue lights of the police around her. A blanket over her shoulders as a nameless cop tried to comfort her, a comfort designed to help her forget what her mother had done.

But nothing could erase that memory.

Charlie winced as one of the medics began sterilizing the wound on his temple.

"We've got to keep moving, Val. Blake Harlow, if he isn't here, he's somewhere. And we've got to catch him before he cuts anyone else up."

"I know."

Valerie looked up again at the window. Miss Armstrong was no longer there, but she could feel her gaze as though she were peeking out somewhere from between two closed curtains.

Your time is coming, Miss Armstrong, Valerie thought. *Soon.*

There would be an inquiry into the orphanage after the arrest. That was for sure.

Valerie noticed that Will had given the young girl a reassuring hug and was now on his way over to them.

"The man you fought with, Valerie, is Mark Derrickson," Will said. "The girl's name is Sarah-Anne. Mark has been disciplining children in the vacant part of the building for some time. All the children are terrified of him and that place."

"What did he do to her?" Charlie asked, his voice grim.

"He would tie Sarah-Anne and a few others up and give them lashes of his belt," Will said with a frown. "Then, he'd leave them there in the dark, telling them that the 'ghosts of Bristlewood' would come for them if they weren't sorry for their bad behavior Sometimes they'd be left for hours. He used the back of the building so no one would hear their screams."

"Did this go on often?" Valerie asked.

"I think so, according to Sarah-Anne at least. Mr. Derrickson was a sort of unofficial disciplinarian for Miss Armstrong when the usual methods didn't get children in line."

"So that old crow, she's involved, too?" Charlie said, the anger clear in his voice.

"It's going to be difficult to prove if Derrickson or the students don't implicate her," Will said. "One thing that's certain is that Mark Derrickson isn't exactly operating on a full tank of gas."

"Is that a professional term, Will?" Valerie smiled.

"That would make sense," Charlie interjected. "I mean, I was just following the guy and he became extremely violent and volatile in an instant. He was unhinged. He could have killed me the way he attacked me from behind."

"He can't have been thinking very clearly if he was going to go through one of his disciplining routines while FBI agents were around," said Will. "I do wonder how long this abuse has been going on for."

"Exactly my thought," Valerie said as the patrol car holding the defeated figure of Mark Derrickson drove off out of the grounds towards the main road.

"You're thinking the same thing, then?"

Valerie sighed and started walking quickly to their car. The others followed.

"Twisted killers like Blake Harlow usually have a violent past. I just wonder if he first experienced it here as a kid."

"That is a thought, you know," said Will, pushing his glasses back up the bridge of his nose as he tried to keep up. "Back at the Culver Institute, you observed, Valerie, that Blake gave special attention to the guard he hated. Perhaps there's a through line from the orphanage to imprisonment."

"He hates authority," Charlie said. "Then we look for someone in authority as his next target. It might give us a chance to get ahead of

44

him if we're right."

Valerie knew they had to move quickly. But to where?

As she opened the driver's door to the car, she turned to her colleagues.

"I get the feeling that we're missing something from his profile," Valerie said. "Something we won't find in any file. But we'll go with the hatred of authority angle for now as motivation. Let's get going."

"Can't I drive?" Charlie asked.

"Not with the knock you just took on your head," Valerie said.

Will's cellphone rang in his pocket. He looked down at the caller ID.

"Can you excuse me for a second? I need to take this." He walked off to speak with the caller.

"We don't have time for this," said Charlie. "What's he doing?"

"I'm not sure. But going by his body language, Will's afraid to tell us something. I think he's going to bail."

"Surely not?"

Will walked back over to the two FBI agents.

"I'm terribly sorry, but I'm afraid I'm going to have to attend to something," Will said, his shoulders hunched as if ashamed. "I'm afraid it's quite urgent."

Charlie let out a laugh tinged with sarcasm. "As urgent as catching a murderer?"

"You can't just abandon an investigation, Will," Valerie said. "You have to be all in, or all out."

"I'm sorry, but it involves a patient of mine," Will said. "He's threatening to kill himself, and I'm the only one who can talk him out of it. But it has to be face-to-face."

"I sympathize, Will," Charlie said, "but if you're going to be part of the Criminal Psychopathy Unit, you might have to stop your practice if it's going to pull you away from an investigation. Especially a ticking time bomb situation like this."

Valerie saw genuine worry in Will's eyes. He was frightened for his patient, and it meant something to him. Life meant something. She respected that dedication.

"Charlie," Valerie said in a soothing voice. "It's okay. We'll take care of things for the rest of tonight, Will. Can you be back tomorrow?"

"Yes, immediately. I hate letting you down."

"Okay, good," said Valerie. "Hold... Hold on..."

Valerie noticed that one of the patrolmen was rushing across the grounds from his car.

"Agent Law!" he shouted, breathless.

"What's wrong?"

"There's been a sighting of Blake Harlow."

"Where?"

"He was seen prowling around 165 Elm Lane. Apparently, he was peering in through a bedroom window."

"My God," Valerie said. She pulled out her notebook and opened it up, looking at something inside.

"What's wrong?" Charlie asked.

"The address," answered Valerie. "It's where Blake Harlow's adopted father lives." She got into the driver's side of the car. "Keys, Charlie!"

"Has a police car been dispatched to the property?" Charlie asked the patrolman as he got into the passenger seat.

"It's on its way," the officer said. "No one's there yet, though. We're actually closer."

Will touched Valerie's arm in a paternal way as though he knew exactly what she would do next. "You both be careful, and please do keep me updated. I wish I could come."

"Thanks, Will," Valerie said. She felt Will's genuine concern, and it was touching. But there was no time to rest in that sentiment.

She turned to the patrolman.

"Grab your patrol car. Come on!"

CHAPTER EIGHT

The smell of the yard made Valerie feel ill. She knew Blake Harlow's father lived inside the house, and by the state of the property, she wondered if he was just as disturbed as his adopted son.

The red and blue lights from the patrol car that had accompanied her and Charlie bathed the dilapidated yard, casting moving shadows beneath the now blackened nocturnal skies.

They had to move fast. Both Valerie and Charlie believed the adopted father might be Harlow's next victim. A man fitting his description had been seen at the property by a neighbor, peering into a window. God only knew what his intentions exactly were, but there was no doubt in Valerie's mind that they would be sick and violent.

Two trash cans were overflowing with garbage next to the lawn and a third had fallen over as Valerie and Charlie walked with purpose along a small garden path, guns drawn, and looking for any sign of the killer.

On the dying, patchy grass, what looked like a rotting chicken carcass had spilled out. Maggots rolled around, feasting on what remained of the bird's flesh. Valerie didn't want to think about what else was making the stench as they reached the porch steps.

Two patrolmen watched nervously from the street, staying back as Valerie had requested. She didn't want them getting in the way of her investigation.

Charlie pointed to a broken window at the side of the house. It had been boarded over at one point, but now the board, stained by rain and dirt, was hanging by a single nail, exposing the inside of the house as if it had been moved aside.

Valerie nodded silently, imagining the creeping, callous figure of Blake Harlow entering the dilapidated house through the gaping hole with murder on his mind.

They'd have to stay sharp.

Stepping up onto the porch, the wood creaked and groaned beneath their feet as the rotten floorboards threatened to give way.

Valerie wondered how such a place could still be standing. Love and care had long since abandoned it.

As Charlie covered her from the steps, Valerie knocked loudly on the door.

They waited. Only silence replied.

Valerie looked at Charlie with concern on her face. The emptiness of that place was seeping into her awareness, and it made her uncomfortable. She had to keep her wits about her. The thought of Blake Harlow hiding inside filled her with dread. She'd never quite faced anyone like that, no one as brutally unhinged.

She knew in her soul that was only a matter of time before their paths crossed. Was the time at hand?

Valerie raised her voice.

"This is Agent Law from the FBI. Mr. Mark Harlow, if you're in there, we believe you're in danger."

A groan now came from inside.

"Someone hurt?" Valerie said, turning to Charlie. She stepped back to kick the door in, but Charlie gently held her arm.

"Wait." He cocked his head, listening.

"What do you hear?"

"Beer cans rattling," he said. "Probably someone waking up and knocking them over… They're coming."

And he was right.

Though her hearing wasn't as good as Charlie's, she could now hear the movement. Footsteps came uncertainly up a hallway until they stopped behind the door.

"Who…," the voice said, groggily. "Who is it? I'm not buyin' anythin'."

"Mark Harlow?" Charlie said loudly.

"Who wants to know?" came the muffled reply from behind the door.

"I'm Agent Carlson, this is Agent Law. We believe you're in danger, Sir. Can you open the door so we can talk, please?"

"Go away. I don't want to talk."

The man on the other side of the door grumbled. Valerie could hear the sound of the floorboards creaking as he turned around to go back to whatever festering beer covered bed lay in his bedroom.

"Your son has killed again and he's on the loose," Valerie said.

There was a pause.

Valerie wasn't certain, but she thought she heard a frail, whispered "no" from behind the door. Imagination or not, a lock turned and then the door slowly creaked open.

From the gap, Valerie could see a dim interior, kept separate from the outside world by the boarded over windows. From around the door, a pale, aged, face peeked out at the two agents.

Valerie felt sorry for the man. His skin was pale and slightly bloated, and his eyes had a yellow tinge to them. There was no doubt that he was in the early stages of liver failure. And by the stench of cheap beer and whiskey, it wasn't hard to reason why.

"Mr. Harlow?" Valerie said in a soothing voice.

"Yeah, that's me," he replied quietly.

"We're here to help you."

Valerie's soft tone brought about a similar softness of expression in the man's face. He looked down at the ground, bashfully, as though he hadn't had a conversation with a woman in many years.

In that moment, Valerie saw only an anxious parent. A father, afraid and uncertain about the world and about what his son might do, powerless to stop him.

Mark Harlow was no monster. He was a man who had been broken by life, drinking the pain away until there was nothing left of him.

When the man looked up, he smiled, and a sea of wrinkles crumpled at the edges of his eyes and mouth. It was a kind smile. Valerie knew that he couldn't have been older than 65, but the booze had made him twenty years older than that.

"Can we come in, Mr. Harlow? We'll only be a minute." Valerie smiled back, and her friendliness acted as a key to enter.

Mark Harlow pulled the door back and waved Valerie and Charlie inside. He was wearing stained, striped, blue pajamas Several holes in them revealed flashes of pallid skin.

"Please, come in here and have a drink," he said, bringing Valerie and Charlie into a living room that stank of stale beer. The floor was littered with empty cans, bottles, and cigarette packets.

Charlie stuck his head out and looked at the back rooms before nodding to Valerie that all was clear.

The old man sat in a lazy boy chair, its spongy innards visible through tears in the fabric.

He grabbed a bottle of whiskey from a cardboard box at the side of the chair and offered it to Charlie and Valerie.

"I keep this for special occasions."

Charlie took the bottle.

"Lagavulin, 21 years, that's not cheap," he said. "I'd love to have a drink with you Mark, but we're on duty, unfortunately."

Mark nodded and put the bottle back in its box. He then rummaged around and found a can of beer. Once opened, he took a gulp, some of it dribbling down his chin and further staining his pajamas.

"Mark, we're worried for you," Valerie said gently. "Blake has killed again. He brutally murdered guards at the Culver Institute. He's escaped, and we have reason to believe he might come here. You haven't heard from him, have you?"

Mark looked up at Valerie.

"You're a pretty young lady," he said. "You shouldn't get yourself involved in things like this."

Valerie wouldn't have put up with talk like that, usually. But there was something disarming about Mark. Like a kind grandfather not knowing that times had changed.

"No... I haven't spoken to the boy in years. I'm ready, though. I knew he'd come for me one day."

"We want to offer you protective custody, Mark. Just until this blows over and we catch him," she said.

"That boy has poisoned my life for so long..."

Mark picked up a framed photograph of a woman on the table next to him. The woman was much younger, in her 30s, and Valerie recognized her immediately from Blake Harlow's file.

"Your wife was beautiful," Valerie said, leaning over and affectionately tapping the top of Mark's hand.

Mark turned his hand and held hers.

"We're both cursed, Agent Law," he said.

"How so?"

"We've got killers in our lives. My family, your prisoners. That gets into ya, there's no doubt about that. Into yer bones. You know, I used to be house proud. The home I had before this one, took care of it. It was a family place. My wife... After that bastard killed her, I became this." Mark gestured to the crushed beer cans and empty bottles around him.

Valerie looked into the old man's eyes and felt the pain there. Behind the kind smile, there was a dark grimace, as if he was in perpetual sorrow. A pain he tried desperately to drown in alcohol.

"So, Mark, you haven't had any contact with Blake since he was incarcerated?" Charlie asked.

Mark laughed.

"The only contact I'll have with him is this." He pulled up his pajama top, revealing two things: an emaciated rib cage and an old revolver sitting in an ill-fitting holster around his waist.

"Can I see the gun, Mr. Harlow?" Valerie asked with kindness in her voice.

"Sure!" Mark's eyes lit up. "You know it's been a while, but I used to be a pretty good shot back in the day."

He pulled out the gun and handed it over to Valerie, who then gave Charlie a knowing glance and passed it over to him.

He held the black handgun in his grip, pulling out the clip. "This is a Mac 50. Haven't seen one of these in a while."

"You know your stuff, Agent... Sorry, my mind is goin' sometimes."

"Agent Carlson, Sir," Charlie smiled. "These were standard issue in the French Army between the 1950s and '70s."

"I've got all the papers for it, if that's what yer worried about," the old man said, pointing at a desk drawer in the corner of the room covered in beer cans and dust. "In there, I think."

"That won't be necessary," Charlie said. "You don't need this gun if you'd let us protect you. We can have some police..."

"No!" the old man barked. "No cops. Not now. They didn't come in time for Jessie. But they shoulda, they shoulda..."

"I'm so sorry, Mark," said Valerie. "I have to ask, but did you have a violent or abusive relationship with Blake?"

"It was *nothing* like that. We got on fine. Even better with his brother, Arthur. You know, it was Arthur we adopted first. Then we found out about Blake and felt it was a sin to keep 'em separated, so we adopted him, too. I wish we'd left him to rot in that orphanage."

"You tried to save him; that was the right thing to do," offered Valerie.

Mark wiped a tear from his eye.

"Didn't do our Jessie much good," he said, pointing back at the photograph. "She had such a good heart. Even when the troubles started, she only saw good in the boy."

"Troubles?" Valerie knew that serial killers often begin exploring their criminality at an early age, but still wanted to know more.

"Yeah." The cold seeped into the old man's voice. "Violent son of a bitch. Seemed cool and calm, well-meanin', too, but then as soon as he was out of eye-shot, he'd break somethin' or harm someone. He terrorized the neighbors, started a fire at the private school we sent him to and even kicked the shit out of another student for nothin'.

51

"Jessie didn't believe any of them. She said her boy wouldn't act like that. Eventually I persuaded her that somethin' needed to be done. So, I got together all the money I could, and we sent him to a proper reform school. That place... What was it called? Jacob... Eh..."

"Jacobson Reform School," Charlie said. "It was in his file. That school had a reputation, didn't it?"

"How were we supposed to know?" Mark said, raising his voice for a moment, then settling back down. "They tell you to send him off somewhere to fix his mind, then when you do it, it turns out the place had violent hazin' and other things, meanin' the kids came out worse than they went in."

"Do you think he blames you for sending him there, then?" said Valerie.

"Maybe. It *was* me. If Jessie had her way, he'd have never gone."

"This is why we think he might be after you," Charlie suggested.

"Was he changed then when he came back home?" asked Valerie.

Mark gulped down the last of his beer and then opened another.

"Uh... Yeah, he was changed alright. Quieter. Seemed happy to be home, though. So happy he wanted to stay in line, so he didn't get sent anywhere else. We took our eyes off him, thinkin' he was sorted... Then..."

"He killed your wife," said Charlie.

"And then some. After that, they said he didn't know what he was doin'. Like it was an illness made him kill those others. The Lithgow woman and those other two guys. But he knew. I know it. I'd love to get my hands on him. My life became this after. I moved out of the old house because I couldn't stand the memory. Her lyin' there. Her guts bleedin' out. Waitin' for the cops. She didn't deserve that. She didn't deserve it."

Mark sobbed for a moment.

"I... I'm sorry. I just don't want to talk no more."

Valerie looked around at the dingy house, the walls stained with nicotine and the carpets soaked in beer.

"Mark, is there anyone else who can help you? Someone you could stay with?"

Mark laughed.

"My other boy is done with me, too. My fault really. I won't stop drinkin', and he's tried everythin' to help. But I think secretly every time he looks at me, I'm a reminder of his mother. I think it suits for me to be out of his life. He can move forward. That ain't a bad thing."

"Any other family or friends?" Charlie added.

"I'm tired. No cops, please. It's been kind of you both to come 'ere. But I need to sleep. If he comes," Mark put his hand out and Charlie gave him the gun back. "I'll take care of him."

Valerie and Charlie stepped into the hallway and spoke in hushed tones.

"We can't just leave him like that," Charlie said. "But what can we do if he won't take protection?"

"Speak to the patrolmen outside," Valerie said. "Ask them to park down the street out of sight so as not to unnerve the poor guy and to call us the minute they see anything suspicious." She tried to bury the guilt deep down, but it was a fire that was never extinguished.

Valerie looked back through the open doorway and watched Mark close his eyes. For a moment, Valerie thought of her own mother sitting alone like Mark, abandoned by her firstborn.

"You, know. I think Mark was a good dad. I can feel it. But Blake Harlow wrecked his life. Now he can barely function."

Charlie sighed rubbing his chin. "Hold on." He turned and walked back into the living room. "Hey, Mark. The gun isn't loaded properly." Charlie made sure the clip was now inserted correctly and came back to Valerie.

"Are you sure that's a good idea?" Valerie said.

"Do you want it on your conscience if the old man was left defenseless and that creep shows up?"

Valerie agreed. "Okay." She then looked at the address in her notebook.

"The brother?" Charlie asked.

"He could be another target. We've got his address now. How's your head?"

"Still on my shoulders," Charlie smiled. "I've got another couple of hours left in me tonight."

Valerie was glad to have Charlie by her side. She pulled out her cellphone to see how far away they were from the brother's address and saw several unanswered messages. Her heart sank. Several were from her sister again and one from her boyfriend.

She couldn't handle either right then. She had to focus. Deep down, she knew she was just putting her personal life on hold, as she always did.

Valerie put the phone back in her pocket without reading anything and walked outside, then through the shadows to their car at the bottom of the drive. Charlie spoke with the patrolmen as she waited in the driver's seat.

Something was wrong.

Charlie's body language gave it away. The patrolman had told him something. Whatever it was, it was bad.

Charlie walked back towards the car shaking his head and looking at Valerie. He got into the car.

"Blake Harlow has killed again."

Valerie's heart raced. She shook the tiredness from her eyes.

"Take me there," she said sounding determined, but deep down she felt as though Blake Harlow was one step ahead of them at each and every turn.

CHAPTER NINE

Valerie couldn't believe her eyes. There, among a quiet suburban area surrounded by houses, a body bag was being carried out of a small Scout hall that doubled as a community center.

Valerie knew who was in that bag. She'd been given the lowdown en route by a county police dispatcher she had a good relationship with.

To her horror, Valerie watched as the body bag was transported into the back of an ambulance.

"God dammit," Valerie said as she exited the car. "Why are they moving the body!"

Charlie raced after Valerie.

"Hey! You!" she yelled at a man in a long raincoat standing by the ambulance. She could tell by the way he was dressed that he was a detective. Homicide most probably, and he'd taken one too many detective shows too literally.

"Can I help you?" the man said as Valerie rushed up to the ambulance.

"I'm Agent Law with the FBI; this is Agent Carlson. Why the hell is the body being moved?"

"Because I've seen all I needed to see and the forensics boys were happy for the body to be moved," the detective said in a thick New York accent.

"It shouldn't have been moved. Not until we had a chance to look at the scene."

"There are photographs," the detective said, a smirk on his face as if amused by Valerie's annoyance.

"I'd wipe that smirk off your face, pal, if I were you," Charlie said.

"And if I don't, let me guess, you'll do it for me?" the detective laughed.

"No," said Charlie. "But Agent Law might."

"Look, this has happened in my precinct," the detective said. "And no Federal Mulder and Scully outfit is going to push me around on my case."

"You're case?" Valerie sighed. "Maybe if you put protocol before

55

pride, we'd actually have a chance of catching this guy, Detective."

A younger police officer walked up to the detective and began explaining some new developments.

"It's weird, Detective," the man said. "The killer set off the alarm in the Scout Hall deliberately."

"The guy is a wacko by all accounts," the detective said.

"A wacko?" laughed Charlie. "Is that a professional term?"

"No, Detective," said Valerie. "He isn't simply a wacko. And I'll tell you exactly why he set off the alarm. The victim, Mr. Alfredo Stanley lives in that house over there." Valerie pointed to a house across the street. "For the last 7 years, Alfredo Stanley has run a Scout group out of this hall here. He's been the custodian. And the man who has just murdered him, was one of his previous scouts."

Valerie didn't have time for anymore smart remarks from the detective. Sometimes she hated liaising with local law enforcement. Usually, things ran smoothly, but every now and then she encountered someone willing to jeopardize an investigation simply because they couldn't handle the FBI having jurisdiction.

Charlie followed Valerie into the back of the ambulance. They both put on latex forensic gloves, which were standard issue.

Carefully pulling back the zip on the body bag, Valerie was stunned by what she saw.

"Another disfigurement," observed Charlie.

The old man's face was cut to shreds.

"Another authority figure, but this time from his previous life. His childhood, in fact. Blake has been busy," said Valerie, thoughtfully. "Look here." She lifted Alfredo's bloodied right hand. His index finger had been removed.

"Hmmm," said Charlie.

"You have a theory?"

"Well, I remember having a summer camp counselor when I was a kid. He used to constantly point his finger in our faces and scream at us for the slightest little thing."

"That's a great idea, Charlie. Maybe Blake removed the finger because it represented authority in some way."

Valerie and Charlie left the ambulance after making all of the observations they could. Valerie was happy to be out of the back of the vehicle. She hated them. It reminded her of several trips to the ER with her mother when she was a kid. Too many trips. Too much pain to think about.

The cool air felt good in her lungs. She walked over to the Scout hall and looked at the scene, but all that was left was a pool of congealed blood on the ground. If there had been anything that would have added to her profile of Blake Harlow, it had been disturbed by the detective's team.

"What now?" asked Charlie as they left the building, back to the red and blue flashing lights outside.

"We better go and see Blake's brother," answered Valerie. "Then I think we should stop somewhere and get some sleep. Stay fresh as possible for tomorrow."

"How would you feel about a night cap? Preferably something strong to wash the taste of today out of my mouth."

"Perhaps," said Valerie. Although she wasn't really in the mood for a drink.

Charlie and Valerie walked past the detective and two of his men on the way to their car.

"Find anything interesting Scully?" he said to Valerie sarcastically.

"Nothing your team didn't mess up, Columbo," retorted Valerie.

One of the police officers laughed. The detective threw him an angry look.

Valerie felt weary. But she had to push on. Blake wasn't stopping his murder spree, so she didn't fell right stopping her investigation. At least, not until her tank was empty.

Getting back into the car, the dark roads ahead beckoned to Blake's brother's house. Valerie felt apprehensive, as if each journey was taking her closer to a man who could only be stopped by a bullet to the head.

CHAPTER TEN

Blake Harlow stopped to catch his breath a couple of miles now from his adopted father's home. The sun was setting. When it was dark, that was when his mind became most disturbed and disjointed.

Escaping from the Culver Institute had been easier than Blake thought.

The plan had been executed flawlessly but rushing to his father's home hadn't progressed as he'd wanted it to. He'd been seen by a neighbor, and, knowing the police and FBI would be on his tail, he improvised an escape route back across the fields before he could face Mark one last time.

Synchronicity, he thought. *The Institute. The Orphanage. Dad's new home. All within a few miles*. There was an opportunity to be done with everything.

With those thoughts of these locations intersecting with his past, Blake felt the oncoming encroachment of *the child*. A manifestation in his mind where he would temporarily shift from a brilliant, intelligent, and devious adult to a simple and impulsive child.

He knew he had to resist the transition. Such a psychotic break could leave him exposed out there, only for the authorities to find him a babbling wreck, crying for his *mommy*.

The adult part of Blake's mind hated the child. But though he could fight against slipping into his former self temporarily, he knew the change would come at some juncture.

Time was of the essence. His plan had to be carried out.

Blake needed to hide somewhere in the fields. He needed to think about his next move. Who would he pay a visit to next? Who deserved it most?

As Blake rushed across an empty country road to a line of low hanging trees, he could feel the old impulses coming again.

The night, he thought. *Always rage with night*.

Blake scrambled over a dry, stone wall into a field, grazing his hands. A sound caught his attention as he fell onto the grass on the other side.

A car.

It was moving through a back road somewhere nearby. The area was littered with those old roads, weaving in out of the hills and then bleeding out into suburbia.

The rumbling of the car engine intensified. It was getting closer.

He couldn't afford for the driver to see him. He couldn't afford for anyone to see him. That was when the killing would start. He was sure of it.

Ducking below the wall, Blake sat there, hoping that it wasn't the police. The car grumbled along a narrow country road that flanked the field.

In the dimming sun, its lights followed the road. For a moment, Blake thought it slowed, as if the driver had seen something important.

Blake clenched his fists, his nails digging into the palms of his hands, drawing blood.

As the car reached its closest point, he could feel the old impulses, the old desires. Just a few feet away, part of the dry wall had crumbled slightly, leaving large chunks of rock on the grass.

"It would be an easy thing," Blake said to himself.

The car was now about to pass.

Blake reached over and grabbed one of the rocks.

"Through the windscreen," he whispered to himself. "In his face. Smash it open."

The car moved within throwing distance. But the rock wasn't thrown.

There was no death, this time. Because a plan was fermenting in Blake's mind.

The driver would never have known how close to death he had come. Instead, he and his car disappeared into the encroaching night as the sun finally dipped beneath the horizon.

Blake dropped the rock in his hands. The driver had been saved by an epiphany.

Blake recognized the road from a distant childhood memory. One of his targets came to mind. He could almost taste the blood as he thought about what he would do to her.

A cool breeze fingered its way across the field towards where he sat, his back against the wall. Only night sounds and night chills now came to him. It was dark. His mind was a torrent.

"I'm near," he thought. "She's near."

As he weaved between the trees, only the moon now lit his way.

The shadows of the leaves and branches poked and prodded the world around him, chattering in the night wind like old broken bones in a grave.

Bushes lashed against his skin. A thorn scratched across his cheek. The uneven ground of roots, clawed at his ankles and heels. But he never stopped. That thought of safety was the only thing that mattered. He knew of somewhere, a place where his mind had last been at ease all those years ago. Before death had come, before murder, torture, and prison.

The woods began to thin, dying off as Blake reached the other side. As if welcoming him to embrace an old friend, they opened up onto the large, manicured lawn of Bristlewood Orphanage.

"Police are near," he whispered to himself, spying two patrol cars near the front of the building and a third to the west side. "But I know this place and they don't."

Blake's feet whispered across the grass as the moon cast long shadows around. Memories were now coalescing in his mind. Thoughts of the past.

His and Bristlewood's past, *intertwined.*

And those thoughts would often result in a strange psychosis. He would soon become mired in his childhood self, losing all concept of his adult years.

He resisted as best he could.

Shaking off the growing doom inside of himself, he moved off, knowing where to hide, which shadows to use as armor against their watchful eyes. Timing his movements to perfection as they periodically looked around.

Blake finally touched the outside of Bristlewood Orphanage, cold in the dark, but the feeling of its grain was a surprising comfort. It had been decades since his childhood hands had touched the brickwork, feeling it and wondering about the ghosts inside.

This set him off.

Like a storm of past experiences washing over him, Blake suddenly lost not where he was, but *when.*

He sat there and thought with childlike simplicity: *Miss Armstrong will be very angry with me if she catches me out of my bed at night.*

Blake looked around and couldn't understand why he was alone. Usually either his brother or some of the other boys were with him when he sneaked out.

This was the conundrum in his mind. A mind so fractured that it would often revert back to a childlike time.

Blake hallucinated going inside as a young boy and being confronted by Miss Armstrong. Her malevolent frown moved towards him, belt in hand, as he was lashed repeatedly against the frame of his bed before he was finally able to sink into the bittersweet relief of his blood soaked bed sheets.

Snap.

And just like that, the storm in his brain had passed. It was something about the grounds in the darkness. They were subtly changed. That change was enough to bring his awareness back to the present.

He remembered a rose bush there when he was a child by the wall, but now it was gone.

Time had moved on, but Blake Harlow's mind was anchored there, anchored by all of the hate and pain he had suffered.

Clarity now replaced the fog, though it would only be a temporary respite from the madness.

She will pay for what she did to me.

Blake followed the feel of the stone to the wooden ledge of an old window.

He knew that window well.

He had sneaked out of it many a time with the others, decades ago. How he hated that place and what they did.

Peering inside, he saw a large room filled with silent bunk beds. Their occupants slept, dreaming childhood dreams and fearing childhood fears.

Pressing his face against the cold glass, Blake could feel the rage of years building up again inside. The world had taken much from him. Perhaps hurting the world was the only way to reply.

She'll be doing her rounds. Like clockwork.

Blake pushed the window up, slowly.

The place smelled the same as it always had, a mix of bleach and old wood. The memories of the beatings, of the horror, came back to him.

A sleeping child stirred in one of the bunk beds as Blake, cold and angry, climbed inside, thinking only of wringing the life out of Miss Armstrong's wrinkled neck.

CHAPTER ELEVEN

It was colder than usual, and it was seeping into Valerie's bones. The moon above cast shadows, and Valerie trusted none of them as she and Charlie approached Blake Harlow's brother's house.

It was on a quiet street corner of an affluent suburb, but silence always made Valerie uncomfortable. She knew it was where deception and malevolence hid easiest.

"It's amazing how people from the same family can be so different," Charlie observed, looking at the pristine yard in front of them.

Blake's adopted father's life was chaotic and broken, but Arthur, his brother, had risen out of the ashes and made a life for himself at least.

"Families are complicated." Valerie was thinking of her sister and mother.

Families were indeed complicated, and she often felt that she would never be able to escape the pain of her own familial trauma. Working cases helped her forget, most of the time. But recently, even work had failed to stop the incessant thoughts about the past that burrowed into her mind and soul. And now her sister's messages were there to bring back the old pain.

You can't escape the past, Valerie. Her sister had told her that three years ago, and the words still stuck in her side like a knife.

"Penny for your thoughts," Charlie said out in the street.

"You'd get short changed," Valerie joked.

"This one's getting to you, isn't it?" Charlie asked.

"The more time we give him," said Valerie. "The more his trail will be littered with victims. If Blake Harlow isn't here already, then I'm hoping his brother can tell us something, anything, that'll help us catch him. Right now, I'm at a loss. This case doesn't sit right with me. It seems simple, but the more we delve into Harlow's past, I feel like our profile might be wrong."

Valerie didn't share a deeper motivation with her partner. Her family history was motivation enough to make sure no one on her watch was hurt by a deranged individual.

Charlie put his hand on a white wooden gate and undid the latch. He pushed the gate open and stepped onto the small path that led up to the quiet house.

"You're just second guessing yourself, Val," Charlie said. "You always do. But that's a good thing. I'd hate to have a partner who rushed to judgment"

"Hold... Hold it right there!" a voice yelled from above, stopping the conversation in its tracks.

Charlie was a cool head, and Valerie was thankful for that. A more inexperienced and jumpy agent would have drawn their gun immediately, but Charlie raised his hands slowly in the air.

They both instinctively looked up and saw a thin man with black hair in his forties leaning out of a window with a frightened look on his face.

He stumbled over his words.

"Who... Who are you?"

"I'm Agent Carlson," Charlie said, taking the lead, as he was the one actually on the man's property. "This is Agent Law. Are you Arthur Harlow?"

"Yes...," the man said, wiping sweat from his forehead nervously. "I... I take it you're here about... Him..."

"Your brother, Mr. Harlow," Valerie said. "He's..."

"Escaped...," the man interrupted, dejection clear in his voice. "I heard it on the news about half an hour ago. Can... Can I see your identification?"

Valerie could feel the man's fear, and it was no wonder.

Both agents produced their FBI shields.

The man squinted.

"I can barely see them from up here. Could... Could you bring them to the door and put them up to the glass?"

"Of course, Mr. Harlow," Charlie said, his voice calm and reassuring.

The two agents walked up onto the front porch, the wood resilient against their weight.

Valerie was relieved that Blake hadn't murdered his brother. He wasn't an authority figure, so he might be spared. But there were no guarantees.

After a moment, Arthur appeared behind a net curtain at the front door and looked at the badges. He finally nodded and unlocked the door.

Arthur was bigger than he appeared at the window, and he was more handsome than Valerie had expected, giving the gnarled features of his brother.

"Quickly!" he said, ushering them inside and then clicking the front door's three different locks.

"You're pretty well secured in here," Charlie said, pointing to the internal motion sensors up in the corners of the ceilings.

"When you've got a brother in a high security psychiatric ward who hates your guts, then you get used to being cautious," Arthur said, moving into his lounge and the agents following.

"Please, have a seat," Arthur said as he pointed to a red leather couch and then sat in a pristine armchair. "Oh... Where are my manners? Can I get either of you some coffee or tea?"

"No thank you, Mr. Harlow." Valerie took out her notebook and sat down. "We're hoping you can help us catch your brother. Do you have any idea about where he might go or hide?"

"Well," Arthur said, patting his brow again. "It's a fairly unusual situation, isn't it?"

"What do you mean?"

"My brother being incarcerated so near to where it all happened before. It's strange."

"Yes, it is," Valerie agreed.

Was it fate? Was it bad luck? There weren't many places like the Culver Institute out there with their experimental therapies. To have had Blake treated in one near where he grew up, that was always going to lead to some catastrophe.

If only others had seen that earlier.

Valerie cleared the clutter from her mind: "We think his proximity makes it likely that he'll visit places or people from his past."

"Do you have a firearm like your dad?" Charlie asked.

"My dad? You've seen him?" Arthur rested his head in his hands for a moment and sighed before looking back up. "How is he?"

"Not good," Charlie offered. "He didn't want any protection. Seems hell bent on taking down your brother himself."

Arthur laughed and leaned back in his chair.

"That's just like him." A worried look grew quickly on the man's face. "I suppose he told you we don't speak?"

"Yes, Mr. Harlow," answered Valerie.

"Please, call me Arthur." He sighed loudly as if releasing a world of

64

stress into the air. "You probably think OI'm cold hearted like my brother?"

"Families are complicated," Charlie said, giving a knowing glance at Valerie.

Valerie pretended that she didn't notice. But Charlie was the only one who had an inkling of her childhood. Though no one knew the full horror.

Rain now came, and it seemed within the blink of an eye that the outside of the house was caught in a torrential downpour. It fingered its way down over the roof and brick and glass, pattering ominously.

"That came on quick," Valerie observed.

"It's like that here," said Arthur. "I like it, though."

"Arthur," Valerie continued. "You've not seen or heard from your brother?"

Arthur shook his head.

"Yes and no."

"What does that mean?" Charlie asked.

"His psychiatrist, Dr. Winters, he had encouraged me to visit him at the Culver Institute. He thought I might help calm him enough so that he'd open up to the doctor."

"And did that work?" Valerie jotted down a thought in her notes.

"I don't know," Arthur replied. "He barely spoke to me during those visits. You'd have to ask Doctor Winters."

"I'm afraid your brother killed Doctor Winters, Arthur," Valerie said softly.

"Oh no… It's starting all over again…" Arthur stood up and began to pace. "If you'd seen what he did when we were younger…"

"Your mother?" Valerie asked.

Arthur nodded mournfully.

"But not just that. Did my dad tell you he killed our dog when we were kids?"

"No, he didn't. But then he was quite inebriated."

"Still drinking then?" Arthur sighed. "I've tried to help him, I really have. But there's only so much you can do. I found my dad's drinking too difficult to deal with; I had to get away. He doesn't even know where I live."

"I understand that. No one is judging." But inside, Valerie was judging. Not just Arthur for leaving his ailing father behind, but judging herself for doing the same thing to her mother. But then, Mark Harlow never attacked his children with a knife.

65

You've left her to rot in that place, Valerie... she thought. Her stomach turned.

Something louder than rain tapped a nearby window.

The color drained from Arthur's face.

"My God, it's him!"

Valerie nodded at Charlie, who then walked over to the window and looked outside. The sound of tapping came again.

"It's the branch from a rosebush," Charlie said. "The wind is getting up."

Arthur let out a gasp of air.

"I'm not usually this jumpy," he said. "But I just thought I was done with Blake, you understand? I'd made a new life, and everything he did, torturing animals, setting fires, killing our beautiful mom, I thought I'd finally put all of that behind me. Getting away from Dad, even though it's not his fault, that was the last connection to Blake.

"Then they asked me to visit Blake... I said no, but then it just worked away at me. Doctor Winters said I might help them understand how he works. Then they might be able to stop future killers like him." Arthur shook his head. "I hope me visiting didn't rile him up to escape."

"Whatever Blake has done," Charlie offered. "That's on him, no one else."

"Again, I have to ask," said Valerie. "Is there anywhere you think he'd go now?"

"The orphanage would be my bet."

"We've already been there, and we've left some cops in the grounds," said Charlie. "If he was going to go there, I think he'd be put off by the security."

"Oh, you don't know him," Arthur suggested. "We used to sneak around those grounds all of the time. He was so clever. He could tell where and when people would be looking so he could go out into the night and then come back without being caught."

"I'm sure it's quite secure," said Charlie.

"Nowhere else?" asked Valerie.

Arthur shook his head. "I supposed I could write down a few places that meant something to him as a kid."

Valerie handed him a piece of paper and a pen. He scribbled down some locations and gave the piece of paper back. "That's about all I can think of right now."

"Arthur," Valerie inquired, "you said that your brother hates your guts. Why is that?"

"Because I went right when he went left." Arthur walked over to a small desk and pulled open a drawer. Rummaging around, he had in his hand some old, yellowed letters bound together with a rubber band.

"Are those from your brother?" Valerie wondered what sort of things a murderous brother would write to his sibling, especially to one he hated.

Arthur nodded in reply. He handed them to Valerie.

"You can read them if you like," he said. "It's all there in his furious handwriting. The rage at being locked up. How I needed to help him. Why it's not all his fault. He thinks there's someone else inside of him, would you believe? Like a split personality."

"Dissociative personality disorder," Valerie said. "It's very rare and often faked. It's sometimes used by violent criminals as an excuse. Do you believe him?"

"I think he's just evil," Arthur replied bluntly. "He might have mental health problems, but most people with mental health issues don't become violent. I think he chooses it all. He's smarter than you think. When we were at boarding school, he set fire to a boy's bed as he slept. He was lucky to get out alive."

"Why does that make him smart?" asked Charlie.

"It was the *way* he did it," answered Arthur. "The boy had gotten into a fight with another kid earlier that day. I could never prove it, but I know Blake did it. And all because he knew the finger would immediately be pointed at the other boy. And it was. That boy was expelled."

"Was Blake angry at either of them for some reason?"

"No, you don't get it with Blake. He did it just because he could, and the fact the two kids had been fighting earlier that day, he knew everyone would think it was because of that and nothing to do with him. If Blake gets a chance to cause harm, especially if he can get away with it, he will do it just for the hell of it."

Valerie took down some more notes and then looked at the letters.

"You can keep those if you need," Arthur offered. "Having them here makes me uncomfortable. I've no idea why I've held onto them."

"Probably because they're the only connection you had left to your brother," said Charlie.

"You do have your dad," Valerie said, looking at Arthur. "Maybe reconnecting wouldn't be a bad idea, if it's not too forward to say."

Arthur rubbed the back of his neck, the stress oozing out of him.

67

"I do want to make sure he's safe, at least while Blake is about," Arthur said. "Are there police in his house?"

"No," answered Valerie. "There's only a patrol car driving by every now and then. It was all we could do without his permission."

"If you don't mind, I think I'd like to go over and check on him," Arthur said, standing up and walking over to a wooden coat stand where he pulled on a long gray jacket. "I'd be happy to answer any other questions later, if that's okay?"

Valerie looked at the letters in her hand.

"I think you've given us quite enough for now. Thank you."

The sound of rain began to lessen slightly, the tapping of the rosebush against the window ceased.

"Would you like us to arrange a car to take you there? You really should have some protection," said Charlie.

"No, thank you," said Arthur. "I'll drive there myself. I think if I turned up with a bunch of police, he'd chase me off for not respecting his wishes. It's best if I go alone. Then maybe I could persuade him to take you up on his offer."

"You're doing the right thing," said Valerie. "It certainly makes us feel better knowing that someone will be with your dad. Call 911 if Blake shows up, and here's my card where you can reach our office."

Valerie and Charlie left the house with Arthur and watched as he got in his car and drove off into the darkness.

"Where to now?" asked Charlie as the rain increased again.

"I think we should get some sleep, there's not much more we can do tonight," Valerie said. "Local law enforcement can keep us appraised if anything develops overnight."

"Will I drive you home?"

"I'm too tired for the journey right now. I think staying at a motel would be a better idea."

"Agreed," Charlie said rubbing the cut on his head. "It's been a rough day."

Valerie handed Charlie Arthur's note.

"Could you let the cops know about these locations and sort out some plain clothed units to watch them for Harlow?"

"I'm on it," said Charlie.

Her hand touched her cellphone in her pocket.

There were messages to be answered.

Her sister's pleading had been biting away at her insides all day.

The sound of Arthur's car had all but disappeared into the distance, but his actions had left an echo in her heart and thoughts.

The man's readiness to go and see his father after all those years, to be there with him in his hour of need, that stirred something in Valerie.

Perhaps it was time for her to face her own tragic past with her mother as well. Valerie promised herself that she would answer her sister's messages and find out what was happening with her mother's incarceration when she got home. But for now, a motel would have to do before the chase continued in the morning.

CHAPTER TWELVE

Valerie, exhausted from the day, pulled up into the parking lot of the tiny highway motel, feeling as if the day would never end. It was dark out now, the lot lit harshly by the cheap floodlights.

After leaving the car, each step felt like a thousand pounds as she walked beside Charlie. They were both exhausted. No amount of coffee would fix that.

Despite the exhaustion, she couldn't stop thinking about the day's events, but she knew that if she didn't rest, she'd start making mistakes.

As much as she wanted to get out there and catch him, her training was telling her when to recharge. And tomorrow, she vowed, she *would* find a way to get him.

She stepped into the cheap motel and went to the desk.

"Need a room?" the cashier asked.

"Separate rooms," Valerie said. "We're colleagues… We're FBI agents."

She looked at the bar in the lobby.

She and Charlie exchanged a glance.

"Want a drink?" he asked. "It might be good to unwind for half an hour before bed."

"Who are you kidding?" Valerie smiled. She knew the case is exactly what they would discuss. "Lead on."

He guided her through the dingy motel to the bar and they took a seat with a view of the parking lot. Charlie ordered some bourbon, neat. Valerie certainly couldn't face a mojito after her drinking session the previous day with her boyfriend.

An Irish cream soothed just enough.

There was no sipping. They downed them quickly. Charlie ordered another each and sat back down at the table.

They didn't say much at first. They just stared at the drinks in their hands.

Valerie's body and mind ached.

The worst part of her job was at night. When a fugitive was still out there doing untold damage to people's lives. She'd spent so many sleepless nights tossing and turning, feeling guilty.

Valerie's brain rarely gave her reprieve. She'd think about the case for some time before sleep took her back at her room. The drink in her hand would help that. But she knew the real reason her thoughts raced at night.

That was when Mom would start to talk strangely.

That was when Mom would get paranoid.

That was when Mom would get unpredictable.

If you spent enough of your nights as a child anticipating something terrible happening, the nights as an adult still held that anticipation. Racing thoughts, indeed.

"Hey," Charlie said from the other side of the bar table. He waved his hand in front of Valerie's eyes as if trying to break a spell. "You okay?"

"Yeah," Valerie sighed, her thoughts of childhood somehow mixing with the case.

Blake Harlow had a terrible childhood, too. Why did I end up wearing a badge and he ended up wielding a knife?

Why does anyone end up good or bad, Val? These were questions she couldn't answer.

"Where do you think the killer is now?" Charlie asked.

Valerie thought about it. She could see Harlow's hulking figure in her mind, moving across unknown terrain. Her mind hadn't formulated a direction for him yet. She had to once more fall back on textbook cases.

"Somewhere out on the highway hitchhiking, if he's escaping the area," she said. "Either that or on his way to another old haunt. I think we're still missing something."

"What?" Charlie said. "What could we have missed?"

"I have a bad feeling we've got his personality traits wrong. It's a hunch, so don't mention it to Will tomorrow. He deals in certainty only," Valerie admitted.

"And if we have the profile wrong, he becomes more unpredictable."

"Exactly," Valerie said, finishing the last of her drink.

"Maybe you *should* mention what you're thinking to Will," Charlie suggested. "He might have some insights. We could give him a call?"

Valerie didn't answer. Her phone had vibrated with another message. She was looking down at the screen.

Another message from my little sis.

"Hey, Val." Charlie's voice had taken a different tone. It was filled with understanding.

Valerie looked up at her partner.

Charlie said, "It isn't like you to be distracted, Val. I've seen you messing with that phone all day. You know I'm here for you if you need a friend, right?"

Valerie nodded, almost letting out a sob but keeping it together.

"Charlie," she said quietly. "If your mom had ever done something terrible to you, would you still be there for her if she needed you?"

Charlie looked thoughtfully at his friend.

"I'd like to think so," he said. "But families are strange. They bring out the best and worst in us. If my mom had been abusive, maybe I wouldn't feel like helping her. But I hope I would."

Valerie listened to her partner, her friend. She'd kept her story to herself for so long. Charlie knew little pieces. He knew that she didn't talk to her mother or sister. But he didn't know why. Valerie had only told him that there had been a fall out.

It was much, much worse than that.

But in that moment, in that dingy motel bar, tiredness coursing through her veins, something stirred inside of Valerie. The case. Harlow's past. Her sister reaching out. It all swirled together in Valerie's head. Just enough to let her pull the mask back, if only for a moment.

"My mom is in a psychiatric unit," she said.

Charlie's brow furrowed in concern. "I'm so sorry. What for, if you don't mind me asking?"

"She's been there for years," Valerie continued.

How much will you share, Valerie? She thought. *Not everything. I can't. Just enough and no more.*

"Things were rough when we were kids," she said. "Me and my little sister. Mom was very ill…"

A flash of her mother standing above her little sister in a kitchen, knife in hand, struck Valerie's mind like a shard of ice.

"It was a tough time," she said. "My sister and I disagreed about how we should help our mom. She wanted to, but I felt I couldn't. There was abuse…"

"I'm so sorry, Val." Charlie reached across the table and held his friend's hand.

"But lately," Valerie said. "Lately, I can't stop thinking about them both. I've built a career, a life, kind of," she laughed. "And I feel like if

I let them in again, my world might crumble. I've kept all that pain at arm's length for so long. I wouldn't know what to do with it.

"My sister started messaging me again. I haven't even looked at them all. Part of me wants to delete it all and block her number. But I don't. It's the guilt."

"It obviously needs to be resolved, Val. I think you need to make a choice one way or the other," Charlie said. "To disconnect for good, or to face the past."

"Which choice would you make?"

"I don't know," answered Charlie. "Probably, I'd…"

Valerie's phone buzzed into life. She looked up at her partner, waiting for him to finish his thought, but he nodded gently.

"Better answer it. You'll get more sense out of whoever it is than me with a few of these in me," he said, pointing to his drink.

Valerie looked back at her phone, half wishing she and Charlie could have continued the conversation, half happy they had been interrupted.

"Hi, Will," she said, answering the phone. "Uh, huh. Yes. Hold on." Valerie cupped the receiver with her hand and turned to her partner. "Will's asking for an update. Let's go to my room and we can chat about the case in private."

A few minutes later, Charlie and Valerie sat in one of the most rundown motel rooms they had ever had the misfortune to see.

"Okay, Will," Valerie said, holding her phone and now a drink of water in her other hand. "You're on speaker."

"Ah," Will said, clearing his throat so loudly, the speaker distorted, making him sound every bit like a stuffy, lovable professor.

Valerie and Charlie giggled at each other.

"How is your patient?"

"Sedated, Valerie. I was able to get him off a bridge, would you believe. Did you have much luck with the brother?"

"Yeah," said Charlie. "The adopted father, too. We've visited both. They're safe for now."

"Oh, thank goodness," said Will. "Anything of note?"

Valerie replied: "Arthur, Blake's brother, he's given us a list of locations in the area that Blake used to like when he was younger. We've sent some plain clothed units to keep an eye on them in case they see anything."

"I see," Will said. Then there was a silence.

"I can practically hear your brain turning, Will," Charlie joked.

"What is it?"

"It's just…," he said. "I've been thinking about a case I had previously."

"Case?" Valerie was surprised. "I thought you had no field expertise."

"Not of chasing a fugitive," Will answered. "But I have extensive experience interviewing psychotic killers once they are in jail."

"That's the hard part," Charlie said, joking again.

"Have… Have you two been drinking?"

"Just a couple to loosen up," answered Valerie. "But I stopped as soon as I got your call. What about your old case, then?"

Will cleared his throat again.

"It was seven years ago," Will said.

Charlie sat back on an old chair as Valerie got comfortable on the bed, still sipping her third Irish cream.

"I'd been asked," Will continued, "to interview a man named David Bannister."

"Oh my God," Charlie said, sitting up straighter. "The Cleveland Butcher?"

"But he wasn't imprisoned until a couple of years ago?" Valerie was confused. "How could you have been interviewing him seven years ago?"

Will's voice sounded nervous. "David Bannister had a history of severe learning difficulties, going back to when he was 14 years old. By this time, he was 38. The police were scouring Cleveland for a serial killer who had already executed 6 people in brutal fashion.

"There were no leads, and the public were getting restless. The detectives on the case were under pressure to find the murderer before he struck again. Finally, they got a break, but an unusual one.

"David Bannister, a man known to have profound learning difficulties, claimed to have seen the killer. Due to his mental condition, detectives had found it almost impossible to get solid details from the witness. I came in to try and extract that information from David.

"We had three interview sessions amounting to at least six hours of conversation. It wasn't until the final hour that I saw something extremely unusual. David was supposed to have difficulty understanding and expressing pleasure, but when I mentioned the mother of one of the victims, I saw, just for the briefest of moments, a flicker at the side of his mouth. Almost a smile."

"What did you do?" Valerie asked, finishing her water on the bed.

"I spoke with the detectives about it, telling them that I had a bad feeling David Bannister was not what he seemed. That he had been faking his condition since he was a teenager.

"But I didn't push hard enough... God I wish I had... Two days later another victim turned up, a young girl. Then three more after that. Finally, he slipped up when he was caught near one of the crime scenes."

"I hear some killers do that," Charlie observed. "They go back to the crime scene to watch the crowds form and take in the worry and spectacle of it all as body bags are removed from the scene. Like they get to relive their kills that way and enjoy the terror they're causing."

"Exactly, Charlie," Will agreed. "One of the detectives saw him standing in the crowd. He was wearing sunglasses and a fake wig, but the detective still approached him. David Bannister ran and was caught."

Valerie felt for Will. It seemed that she wasn't the only person tortured by guilt.

"Will," she said, sitting up from the bed. "You can't blame yourself for him slipping through the detectives' fingers."

"But I do blame myself, Valerie," he said. "Four more people died, and I could have stopped it. I just didn't follow my observations with enough conviction. If I had pressed the matter, maybe he would have been held under suspicion of being involved. Instead, he went back out onto the street. He must have loved that."

"Why did he approach the police and say he'd seen the killer?" Charlie asked, still working his way through his last bourbon.

"Arrogance and gamesmanship," Will answered. "He loved being that close to us without us knowing. And he was good at the act because he had a quite brilliant, though warped, intellect. You'd have to, to have been able to keep up the pretense of having learning difficulties for more than two decades."

"Do you think this relates to our case, Will?" asked Valerie.

"Well... I've been perusing Doctor Winters's notes on Blake Harlow again, and I do wonder. He described the man as utterly unhinged, but almost so much that he couldn't be considered a rational killer; instead he was more of an impulsive one. But does that sound to you like someone who could break out of a maximum-security psychiatric facility?"

"No," said Charlie. "To lure the guards in for the kill, get Doctor

75

Winters's keys and ID to escape the ward, and then to use the ventilation system two corridors away the way he did to get out, that requires a lot of skill and foresight to not get caught."

"Exactly," Will continued. "I just wonder, could all of these notes actually be worthless? Could we be dealing with a man so calculating, that he's created a fake set of personality traits to fool the doctors."

"Oh my God." Valerie was shocked by the implication. "Someone capable of faking who they are for so long, any profile of them would be useless. We'd be unable to guess their next move, and worse, we'd be flying in the dark hoping we stumbled across them."

"When I read these notes," Will said. "It made me think of David Bannister. And I had to call. I'd hate to hold anything back and it result in something terrible happening. Anyway, it's worth keeping in mind."

"Reminds me of the Clawstitch killer," Valerie said with a worried expression.

"Clawstitch?" said Will. "I can't say I'm familiar with that case, was it recent?"

"Yeah," Valerie said, her voice sounding distant. "It was pretty recent. Charlie and my first case together in fact."

"Don't remind me," sighed Charlie.

"That bad, eh?" asked Will.

"The one that got away, Will," said Valerie. "Nearly cost me my job. It's taken me some time to come back from it. I'll tell you about it another time, but I can say one thing: If Blake Harlow is a quarter as smart as the Clawstitch killer, we'll be lucky if we ever catch him."

"If Blake's so calculating," said Charlie. "Do you think he could deliberately lead us on. You know, make us think he's after his family when he has another target? He was seen prowling around his father's house, but then he must have left. Was he seen on purpose? We start to circle around his family while he slips into somewhere else for another kill?"

"I wouldn't put anything past him at this point," said Valerie.

"Me neither," said Will. "I just wanted to get this off my chest. I couldn't sleep otherwise. I appreciate you listening to me. I'll leave you both to get some sleep. I'll be back as soon as I can."

Will felt so fragile in that goodbye. Valerie wondered if anyone, even the experts, were ever truly together. Did everyone have their own private neuroses? Even, madness?

She shook the thought from her mind.

"Thanks, Will," Valerie said as the call ended. She lay back down on the bed and closed her eyes to think.

Where are you, Harlow?

"This case is going to mess with my head," Charlie said.

"Yeah…" But for once, Valerie was starting to drift off to sleep.

"Goodnight, Val," Charlie said quietly.

She heard him leave the room, and that was then the darkness of sleep came. But it wouldn't be a restful night. Valerie was about to face something in her dreams she dearly did not want to see.

CHAPTER THIRTEEN

Miss Armstrong walked the halls of the orphanage, closing the shutters against the lashing wind and rain of the dark night. It was a satisfying feeling, slamming the shutters and closing the school off to the world. If she had her way, these kids would never get out--and visitors would never get in. The orphanage was her domain and hers alone, filled with rooms, furniture, and children. All hers to control as she saw fit.

She marched down the hall, her heels clicking and echoing in the night, looking for any infraction, any tiny thing out of place. She hoped for an infraction--there was nothing she loved more than disciplining these children. They all deserved it.

And she was angry. She needed to vent it somehow. Those agents and that damned psychologist. They were meddling in how she ran the orphanage, and that would not do. That would not do, *at all*.

Reaching one of the girls' dormitories. Miss Armstrong looked in to see a girl out of bed. She was looking out one of the windows into the black night. The rain dripping down the glass. She wore a thin cotton nightgown and she looked cold. Her vulnerability offended Miss Armstrong almost as much as her breaking of the rules.

The girl's short blonde hair was matted, and her small fingers clung to the sill.

Miss Armstrong was going to give her a good slap for this. She stepped inside the room.

"What are you doing?" she asked sternly. "You know the rules. You're not allowed out of bed for any reason other than to use the bathroom."

The girl didn't answer, and Miss Armstrong strode up to her.

"How dare you not respond to me, you insolent little girl."

She put a hand on the girl's shoulder and pushed her around to face her.

The girl's face was streaked with tears. She was thin, her eyes hollow and her lips pale. Miss Armstrong didn't recognize her, but then again, she couldn't remember the names of any of the children.

"You should be asleep," she said. "It's late. What do you think you're doing?"

The girl was frail. She looked no older than eight.

"I want to go home," the girl whispered. "My aunt can look after me."

A memory came to Miss Armstrong. The girl was a new arrival just that day. The girl's aunt was her only living relative, and she had recently taken so ill it was impossible for her to care for the girl any longer.

"It doesn't matter what you want," Miss Armstrong said. "Your aunt isn't long for this world. Get to bed or you'll be out on the street with the rest of the trash."

They were all filthy urchins with eyes filled with hunger and hopelessness.

"My parents are dead," the girl said, her voice cracking. "You're mean."

"Shut up!" Miss Armstrong said, raising her hand above the child as if to strike.

The girl cowered.

"Your parents had it easy, Child. I am now the one left to deal with you. Get. Back. In. Bed. Now!"

Miss Armstrong could feel the other children pretending to be asleep in their beds, fearing they might get picked on next. That made the old lady feel good. They needed to fear her. Fear was the best antidote to any hint of rebelliousness.

The girl stepped to the side, sobbing, and then shrank back into her bed.

"Good," said Miss Armstrong. "And if I ever catch you out of bed again, you'll get far worse."

Miss Armstrong walked out the room and slammed the door, satisfied at another job well done.

Miss Armstrong continued walking. There was only one more dormitory to check on before she could finally go to bed. It slept a few young boys, most of whom were troublemakers of the worst kind, in her eyes at least.

She moved through the empty, echoing corridors, and then stood at a closed door. Pressing her ear up against it, she listened. Someone was moving inside.

Miss Armstrong swung the door open violently. But to her dismay, all of the boys were in bed either asleep or pretending to be asleep. One blanket twitched slightly. It was a young boy, Thomas. He was always preyed upon by the others. How she hated his inability to stand up to the bullies.

She fervently believed children should sink or swim. And he was sinking.

But now, Miss Armstrong could feel tiredness creeping into her eyes. She wasn't as young as she used to be, and the day had been a stressful one. She would leave reprimanding Thomas for now and go to bed, hoping that the snooping police would be off of the orphanage's lawn in the morning. Though she suspected they would be there until Blake Harlow was caught.

Miss Armstrong remembered him, too. She'd had to discipline him many times. How such a sniveling wretch could cause such chaos, she'd never understand.

Miss Armstrong kept walking, aggravated, turning down another corridor towards her quarters--when she heard it.

A noise.

It was out of place here, and she sensed trouble.

Not another leak. This place is falling apart.

It was the sound of water dripping somewhere nearby.

Ugh, if I wake up to a flooded room, there'll be hell to pay.

She thought this just as she stepped forward and her footfall made a strange noise. It was wet, a slap against the cold, hard floor.

Looking down, she saw that the floor was wet.

A small layer of water was slowly fingering its way along the floor. She followed it with her gaze to a door.

An old dormitory not currently used. At least none of the brats could complain about it.

Miss Armstrong sighed.

"I better check, anyway," she grumbled to herself, thinking about the inspection that Agent Law had requested for the orphanage. The last thing she needed was for anyone to find water and damp in the rooms and hallways.

Stepping forward, Miss Armstrong's footsteps continued to slap hard against the water. She opened the door where it was coming from and felt the water soaking into her shoe.

She let out another grumble and stepped inside the room.

Little did she know that was the last sound she'd ever make.

A man moved swiftly out of the shadows and thrust a shard of broken glass straight into Miss Armstrong's neck. As she fell to the ground, she recognized the man. Blake Harlow had come for revenge. That revenge was swift and brutal.

Miss Armstrong felt her body being dragged along the floor as the blood oozed from her neck until finally, she entered an abyss of darkness forever.

CHAPTER FOURTEEN

Valerie was having a dream, and it was not a pleasant one. At first, everything was black. When she opened her eyes in the dream, she saw the dull gray walls and knew instinctively where she was.

The room was one of hundreds, each a prison for the building's countless patients.

Some screamed in the distance, others rattled the beds to which they were tied, and outside in sterile corridors, the feet of orderlies, nurses, and doctors echoed, free to roam and to judge and to sedate.

A muffled voice then sounded to Valerie. It was coming from the next room. She put her ear to the wall and heard that it was her mother talking.

"A broken mind is worse than a broken arm," the voice said.

"I just want to go home," said another voice, this one her father's.

"I tried to protect both of you. I thought that if you were separated, you'd be safer," said her mother. "But look what happened! I ended up here!"

"I'm sorry," said her father. "I'm so sorry."

"You're sorry? You're sorry! I'm the one who had to watch you both suffer. I'm the one who had to choose between you and our children! Don't leave me here…"

"It's too late. I have to let you go."

"Please don't—"

Valerie heard a sharp crack, like a snapping bone through the wall. Her mother cried out in agony, and the only word that could be recognized through the screams, was "Valerie."

"I'm coming Mom!"

Valerie leaped to her bare feet and ran to the door. When she smashed her fist against it, she was surprised that it slowly opened.

Stepping out of her room, she found herself in a dimly lit corridor. Now, though, the place was silent. The fluorescent lights were flickering, and the air was filled with dread.

The screams continued.

Valerie had to get into the next room to save her mother.

The corridor was suddenly plunged into pitch black.

The lights had failed. Fear began to course through her veins.

Running her hands along the cold walls, Valerie felt that the corridor was now unfathomably long, as though space and time were being twisted to keep her from the screams of her mother.

She turned another corner and saw the door to her mother's room as one of the overhead lights flickered back to life.

She was so close.

Valerie ran towards the door, but then crashed into a looming figure that appeared out of thin air. They both fell to the floor. She felt a tight grip around her throat, choking her.

An almighty crunch sounded, and the building shook violently. A large crack splintered underneath where Valerie struggled against her attacker and then fingered its way up the nearest wall.

The fluorescent lights above broke free from the ceiling and swung from side to side, casting grotesque shadows all around.

As the man on top of her increased his grip, Valerie felt death nearing.

She recognized him.

The murderous face of Blake Harlow peered down on top of her.

With all of her might, she kicked out in a blind panic, until she felt Blake Harlow's grip loosen.

Throwing him to the side, she crawled towards her mother's door, the screams still echoing.

Turning the handle, the door opened.

At first, she thought there was another light swinging from the ceiling of the dim room. But it was not. It was a withered body, and it wore the decaying face of Valerie's mother.

"No!" Valerie screamed.

She reached the body and tried in vain to somehow stop her mother's death, but death had already come.

Valerie sobbed.

Blake Harlow laughed from the corridor.

And Valerie's mother opened her dead eyes.

"You left me here to die," she said with anger and spite in her voice.

Valerie woke in a pool of sweat. She was still in the motel room. A neon light bathed the bland place in blue beams and shadows.

She wasn't sure how long the phone had been ringing.

"Hello?"

"Hello, Agent Law?"

Valerie knew the voice immediately. It was her boss, Jackson Weller.

"What's happened?" Valerie tried to expunge the memory of her nightmare.

"There's been another murder, Agent Law," Jackson said. "And it happened under our watch."

*

Police cars encircled Bristlewood Orphanage, many more than had been left on guard.

Miss Armstrong was dead, that much was certain. Her throat slit with a shard of broken glass.

Will Cooper, who Jackson had also called about the murder, came walking out of the orphanage front doorway and greeted Valerie and Charlie.

"How the hell did he get in, Will?" Valerie said, frustrated.

"He knew these grounds better than anyone," Will answered. "He was able to evade the police outside, then he broke in and killed Miss Armstrong."

"Why would Harlow risk getting caught?" asked Charlie.

"Perhaps his mental condition has made him reckless," mused Valerie.

"No," Will replied. " His actions are too deliberate. I believe he meant to end up here, whether consciously or not. His past is too great a pull."

"His anger at the orphanage and Miss Armstrong too...," offered Charlie.

"At least we now know he's heavily motivated by revenge," said Valerie. "What if he's still here? Has a full search of the building and grounds been carried out?"

"The homicide detective in charge of the scene told me there was no sign of Blake Harlow. I think he's already gone," Will replied. "He won't come back here anymore."

"Yes, his work is done," said Valerie. "Psychopaths often have a deep-seated urge to extinguish pain from their past. That's why serial killers who are emasculated by their mothers as children often target women. In effect, they're murdering their mothers over and over each time they kill."

"In this case," Will speculated, "the killer is going directly to the source. He's not killing proxies or representations of the people who have wronged him."

"He's going after the real thing," Charlie said.

Will led Valerie and Charlie into the orphanage, through some narrow corridors until they reached a dorm room.

Miss Armstrong's body lay lifeless on the floor as a police photographer took pictures for later study.

A large shard of glass stuck out of Miss Armstrong's neck, her eyes were wide-open and lifeless, and her skin was even paler in death than it had been in life. Several large gouges had been cut into her cheeks and nose. Blood had pooled around the body on the floor.

On the nearest bed, blood had been smeared over the sheets by maddened, murderous hands.

Valerie knelt down to inspect the corpse.

Miss Armstrong's hands were covered in blood, as if she'd tried to stop the wound from bleeding.

"She was taken by surprise," Valerie said. "Otherwise, she'd have defensive cuts on her hands as she tried to fend the killer off."

"What does that tell you?" Will asked.

"If I may," Charlie interjected. "Defensive reactions are measured in milliseconds. The killer must have been waiting to be able to kill so quickly without Miss Armstrong reacting. Look around here; none of these beds have been slept in. This is an unused dorm room. He was hiding in here for a reason, and he lured Miss Armstrong in deliberately, waiting to strike as soon as the door opened. Look."

Charlie pointed to blood splatters a couple of feet away by the door frame.

"Yes," Will said, rubbing his brow. "So he waited, struck, then pulled her over here and laid her down. Why?"

Valerie was in deep thought. She noted that the killer hadn't just attacked her once. There were other wounds across the body, made during a frenzy of violence.

She looked up at Charlie and Will. "She was murdered before she was mutilated. The first wound is the one to the neck. The other wounds are postmortem."

Valerie then looked to the blood smeared across the bed, with Miss Armstrong's body lying on the floor just in front of it.

"This is a sacrifice," Valerie said with certainty. "She was offered up to this specific dorm bed."

85

"Wait," said Charlie. "You don't think this was his when he was a kid?"

Valerie nodded.

"Interesting theory," said Will. "But why would he sacrifice Miss Armstrong and lay her blood on the sheets."

Standing up, Valerie let out a sigh and looked at Miss Armstrong's body. She had seen enough blood for a lifetime. But she knew there would be more if they didn't catch Blake.

"He sacrificed Miss Armstrong to his younger self," Valerie said, motioning to the body and then to the bed. That bed, if it was his, would have been his only place of solace. A place where a beat-up kid, an abused kid, would lie at night and perhaps dream of escaping this terrible place."

"Or dream about retribution," Will said. "And all these years later, he's done just that. I wonder how he lured Miss Armstrong here?"

"Noise maybe?" said Charlie. "She'd have known this room was vacant."

"And if Miss Armstrong is... was the person I think she was," said Valerie. "She would have had a schedule you could have set your watch to; think of how she made us wait outside her office. And I doubt that schedule would have changed much, if at all, over the years."

"He knew where she would be walking in the evening; then," Charlie said, coldly, "he lured her in here, probably heard her familiar footsteps."

"Now what?" Will asked.

Valerie thought for a moment.

"We should speak with some of the kids and staff to see if they saw or heard anything."

"But we know that it's Blake Harlow already?" Will asked, confused.

Valerie found it easy to forget how green Will was when it came to work in the field. But she was happy to explain.

"Will, sometimes the smallest detail can lead to an arrest," she said. "When we're chasing a dangerous fugitive, we need to leave no stone unturned. Often, it's through interviews and questioning that we turn up some piece of information we didn't think of."

"Yeah," Charlie agreed. "It would be good to know if Blake Harlow did or said anything that suggests his next move. It'll all depend on whether they *did* see anything."

"Christ, I hope they didn't," said Will, looking mournfully at Miss

86

Armstrong's   vacant   stare.

CHAPTER FIFTEEN

"I didn't see anything, Miss. I swear," the young girl said.

Valerie's heart sank. This was the 17th child they had interviewed, and time was ticking.

Valerie looked at Charlie and Will, both standing nearby in the antiquated, wood-paneled office on the ground floor of Bristlewood. They looked like forlorn figures, too.

She could feel their disappointment at the children and staff's responses to their questions.

"Thank you, Lacey," Valerie said to the girl. "Now you run along and try to get some sleep. There's nothing to worry about now."

The girl nodded, smiled, and then left the room, running into the corridor nearby that was still lined with children waiting to be interviewed.

"No scream. No witnesses. No leads," Valerie said with a sigh. She began to think that the orphanage was now a dead end.

"Should we cut our losses and let local law enforcement do the rest of the interviews?" Charlie asked.

"Yeah," answered Valerie.

"If he's this stealthy, he could be anywhere," Will said.

Valerie stood up and walked out of the small office they had been using to question the sleepy children one by one.

Outside in the corridor, there were another thirty children or so waiting to be seen.

Charlie walked over to a police officer standing guard.

"Tell Detective Gingrich that he and his team can take over the interviews for now."

The officer radioed his superiors as Valerie, Will, and Charlie walked along the corridor towards the exit.

The sea of young faces looked up at them as they passed, and Valerie felt for them, up during the night, their world upturned again. Miss Armstrong may have been cold and mean, but she was the only constant in their traumatic lives.

Now she was dead.

Valerie smiled at the children as she walked. She wanted to put her arms around each of them and tell them everything was going to be okay.

Something then caught her eye.

A small boy was covering his face with his hands.

It was a classic aversion tactic, and in one so young, Valerie knew that a child would physically try to hide when they had something they didn't want revealed.

Valerie moved over to the young boy and spoke gently.

"Hi, my name's Valerie. What's yours?"

The boy peeked out from between his fingers.

"Thomas," he said, timidly.

"Well Thomas," said Valerie. "How would you like a nice big hot chocolate?"

Thomas slowly withdrew his hands from his face, revealing a pale complexion. He was trembling but nodded.

Valerie took his hand and slowly led him back to the room where they had interviewed the other children. Charlie asked one of the cops outside the room to get a hot chocolate for the boy, and within minutes it was in his hands. He sipped it, a smile on his face for the first time since Valerie had laid eyes on him.

"Thomas," Valerie then said. "Did you see anything here tonight?"

The smile quickly disappeared from his face, and the boy shook his head, staring down at his hot drink.

"It's okay if you did," offered Valerie.

"I didn't see anything," he finally said. "But I heard something."

"What did you hear?"

"A voice."

"From where?"

"Through the wall from my bed." Thomas took a big sip of hot chocolate.

"Good stuff, isn't it?" Valerie asked.

"Yes," the boy said now with glee. "Miss Armstrong doesn't let us have treats."

"Well," said Valerie. "I know it's difficult to understand what's happened here tonight, Thomas. But me and my friends here," Valerie pointed to Will and Charlie. "We're here to make sure whatever bad things happened tonight, and whatever bad things have been happening here before then... That nothing bad happens anymore. Do you believe me?"

89

The boy nodded.

"One of the older boys says Miss Armstrong got a piece of glass in her neck," Thomas said, suddenly.

Valerie looked at Charlie and Will with concern.

"Probably overheard one of the cops discussing it," Charlie said.

"Or one of the other staff, perhaps," added Will.

Valerie turned to Thomas.

"Something bad happened to Miss Armstrong," Valerie said.

"She's bad. Maybe she deserved it," Thomas said.

"No one deserves that, Thomas. But even if you feel she did, the man who did this, he might hurt someone who doesn't deserve it somewhere else. We need to catch him before that happens. We're like detectives."

"Like Sherlock Holmes?" Thomas asked, a gleam in his eyes.

"Yes, like Sherlock Holmes."

"My dad used to read me and my sister those stories... Before the fire."

Valerie held back a flurry of emotion. It didn't take much for her to guess why the boy was at the orphanage. She couldn't bear to think of a child alone after something like that.

"I'm sorry, Thomas."

Thomas sipped his drink.

"Do you want to be like Sherlock Holmes and help us solve this case?" Valerie asked.

"You mean catch the man who did it?"

"Yes, exactly. I'll be your Doctor Watson," Valerie said with a wink. "How about you tell me what you heard and let's see if we can make sense of it."

"Okay... There was a man talking through the wall," Thomas said, wiping some hot chocolate from his chin. "He was talking to himself."

"And what was he saying?"

"He kept saying something over and over again, like 'can't go back,' over and over." Thomas looked keenly into Valerie's eyes. "Valerie, can I tell you something?"

"Yes, anything."

"The voice. The man. He sounded like one of the kids here. He was frightened."

Valerie didn't have the heart to tell Thomas that Blake Harlow *was* one of them. A previous orphan, who perhaps once had sat like Thomas did, with innocent eyes and innocent thoughts, only to be corrupted by the world, by people like Miss Armstrong.

"Did he say anything else?"

"He was whispering 'can't go back,' then he said something about a storm at a school. I don't know what that was. But he sounded scared."

"A storm at a school?" Will repeated from across the room. "Thomas, have you any idea what that meant?"

"Maybe the weather was bad or somethin'," the boy replied.

"And that was everything?" Valerie asked.

The boy nodded, but Valerie noted something else. When he nodded, he looked down at his feet.

"You know, Thomas," said Valerie. "This is a safe place for you. You can tell us if something else happened."

"I don't want to get into trouble. If Miss Armstrong finds out..."

It was then that Valerie realized the boy didn't fully understand what had happened. And why should he have? It was difficult enough for an adult to comprehend.

"Miss Armstrong won't be at Bristlewood orphanage anymore, Thomas. And no one will get you into trouble. If anything, you'll get another hot chocolate when you want it."

That seemed to do the trick.

"We're not supposed to get out of bed," Thomas said. "But I did. I went through to the next room to see who was there. I know it sounds weird, but I was confused at the start. I thought he sounded like a kid. And he started crying, asking for help. I wanted to help him. No one helps around here. My dad always told me to help people."

Valerie's heart broke at that last sentence. Thomas was an orphan, but he still carried the love of his parents in his actions.

"And what did you see?"

"I was scared. I saw a man crouched in the corner of the room with his head in his hands; he was crying, but his voice sounded much younger than he looked, if that makes sense? He was acting like some of the kids who just get here."

"You're a lucky boy he didn't see you," Charlie said.

"But he did see me," Thomas said. "He stood up and told me not to be scared, just like you did, Valerie."

Valerie's skin crawled at the comparison.

Back in her academy days, she'd been told that profilers, the best profilers, often shared some traits with those they were profiling. It was why they were so good at it.

Valerie refused to believe that.

91

"What else did the killer say to you, Thomas?"

"That he was sorry," Thomas said. "That he didn't like hurting people. I didn't know what he meant. He kept saying he was sorry. Something inside him made him do it. Then he told me not to tell anyone about him."

"He said 'sorry,'" Will said, rubbing his chin in deep thought. "Now that is interesting. Could it be that there's a part of Blake Harlow's psyche that has genuine remorse?"

"I got scared then when he moved across the room to me," Thomas said. "I ran back into the dorm and hid under my blanket. He didn't follow me."

"And that's everything?" Valerie asked, softly.

"Yes," Thomas said, this time looking up directly at Valerie.

She knew he was telling the truth.

"You go back to bed now, Thomas," Valerie said sweetly. "And dream nice things. The world isn't always bad. It'll be much better here now, in the future, I promise."

Thomas slid off his chair and put the empty mug on a table. Then Charlie led him out of the room, handing him off to one of the officers, before returning to consult with Will and Valerie.

"This sign of empathy seems out of character," Charlie said. "Blake Harlow's more complicated than we thought."

"And that makes him more dangerous," Will said. "It makes me think of the Weepy Voiced Killer."

"I'm not familiar with that one."

"Paul Michael Stephani," Valerie added. "He would make a call to the police after leaving his victims to die, full of remorse and crying. It's one of the only instances where a serial killer genuinely seemed to be capable of overwhelming empathy, sadly only after killing and venting whatever rage he had."

"This makes him far more unpredictable then, if he doesn't follow usual killer behaviors," Charlie pointed out.

"Definitely," said Valerie. "In fact, he might not even be a psychopath, technically. He's shown remorse, and he's talking about something inside of him making him kill. That makes me wonder if we're dealing with a far more complex set of mental illnesses."

Will was silent for a moment.

"What do you think, Will?" Charlie asked.

But Will did not respond. He was deep in thought.

"Will?" Valerie prodded.

"Great," Charlie said sarcastically. "We broke him. We'll need to order another."

"Hmm?" Will said, snapping out of it. "Sorry, I was just thinking about something Thomas said."

"What?" asked Valerie.

"He heard Blake Harlow say something about not being able to go back, and then something about a 'storm at a school.' The walls would have muffled the voice. Could it be that Blake was talking about his reform school?"

"That could be his next target," Valerie said, her voice grim. "If there's anyone still there who caused him pain as a child, he might kill again."

Charlie pulled car keys out of his pocket.

"I'll drive."

CHAPTER SIXTEEN

Valerie knew that the Stevenson Reform School had a terrible past, and, as Charlie drove her towards its towering black gates, she instinctively felt a foreboding in her bones. The grim, dull skies above were a clouded companion to that apprehension, bearing down on her from a great height.

"It looks more like a prison than a school," she observed.

"I suppose in some way," Will said from the backseat of the car, "it is a prison. A place where children can be rehabilitated from pathological behaviors That's not necessarily a bad thing."

Will was an academic, so Valerie expected him to try and see the best in treatment centers and corrective institutions; but although she knew they were necessary some of the time, she often worried that they created malevolent self-fulfilling prophecies. Label a kid a criminal, and they'll play the role like a seasoned actor.

Charlie had kept the headlights on for a portion of the drive. Even though it was daylight, the clouds above had snuffed out much of the sun.

The headlights of the car caught something in front of the gates as they neared. It was a tall, balding man in an immaculately pressed pinstripe gray suit.

"Looks like we have a welcome party," Charlie sighed. "Never a good sign."

"How so?" Will asked.

Valerie felt sorry for Will. For all his talent as a psychologist, he really was naive to field work.

"It usually means we're going to be kept at arm's length away from anything that might help."

Charlie parked the car and got out into the cool air with Valerie and Will quickly following. Valerie felt the notebook in her pocket. It was too empty. She needed more leads on Blake Harlow and hoped the grim facade of the Stevenson Reform School contained them beyond the gates and within.

"Hi, I'm Agent Law," Valerie said, approaching the man with her hand outstretched. "We're here about Blake Harlow."

"Yes, your office called ahead," the man said, shaking Valerie's hand. "A man named Jackson Weller seemed quite assertive about us assisting."

Valerie noticed that the man had a strong grip, but his voice was far more timid, almost gentle. It was far removed from the coldness of Bristlewood Orphanage and Miss Armstrong.

"My name is Chester, Chester Quill, I'm the custodian of the Stevenson Reform School."

"Agent Carlson," Charlie said, then pointed to Will. "And Dr. Cooper. Could we take this inside, Mr. Quill? We're involved in a Federal manhunt, and it would be better to discuss things in private."

"Yes, of course," he said, turning and opening the large gates. "But one thing."

Valerie knew there was always *one thing*. A catch to be caught.

"We've done everything we can to remove the school from the crimes of its former staff," Chester said. "I'm sure you're aware of the abuse scandal that was uncovered here... But people are still looking for excuses to shut us down, so I just wanted to ask for discretion as much as possible."

"We're not intending on causing any unnecessary fuss," Will offered. "We just want to know about Blake Harlow's history here."

"Of course," Chester said, leading them through the gates. "I'll do everything I can to help. I just don't want the children disturbed by what is, by definition, a disturbing turn of events. It's not every day that a previous student is on the loose and capable of murder."

News travels fast, Valerie thought.

They walked up a graveled path to the steps of a large gray building with sharp angles and sterile character.

"'70s architecture?" Will asked.

"Yes," Chester replied. "Can't say I'm a fan. Far more imposing than it needs to be, especially when we should be nurturing children here." He turned and smiled at Valerie. "You'll find we've moved on from the harsh days of the past where our children were treated like criminals."

Although the man seemed sincere, Valerie was skeptical. *You might have good intentions*, she thought. *But not everyone does.* For a moment, Valerie thought of her mom in another type of institution. What were the intentions of the doctors there? Were they good? Did they care for her?

95

Valerie didn't know. She hadn't visited in years.

The four figures walked through two swing doors into the lobby, which was much smaller than Valerie expected.

She was aware of the sudden feeling of being in a contained space. She couldn't help but wonder what it was like for the children who passed through there. Children often felt small as it was; that's what made them act out. To feel big. The reform school had been seemingly designed to make them feel even smaller. Valerie doubted that was very productive in rehabilitating them.

The door behind shut with a clank, echoing in hidden chambers and corridors. Valerie half expected to turn around and see jail bars rising up from the ground all around them to cage them in.

"I'm aware of the abuse scandal two decades ago," Valerie said, trying to focus on the job at hand. "I believe Blake Harlow was here at that time?"

Chester nodded, uncomfortable in his demeanor.

"I can't help but think," the custodian said, "that he wouldn't have turned into such a brutal serial killer if the previous staff here had been... kinder."

"We're not here to point fingers," Charlie said. "But do you know much about Blake's time here at the reform school? Anything you can give us will help us build a better picture about what his next move might be."

Chester chewed his lip, clearly contemplating the implications of what he was about to say.

"I know his file very well, Agent Carlson, and I've been going over it again and again in my head because of his escape. It's grim reading."

"Did it give you any further insight?"

"Given what I've found out, I can honestly say that it's a miracle he didn't turn out to be one of the most dangerous criminals in American history. I was only a teenager at the time, of course, and not working here," Chester said. "But since I came here as custodian a few years ago, I have come to know that he was one of the worst cases that has ever come through the reform school's doors."

Chester stepped across to the front desk where a fresh-faced secretary was busily typing. He nodded to her, and she quickly handed over an old brown folder that was thick and tattered.

"You'll have to forgive me, Agent Law," he said. "But we had a flood a few years ago in the basement, and some of the older files were damaged. But most of Blake Harlow's notes are here."

96

Valerie took the folder and perused its yellowed pages. Page after page of reprimand, punishment, and a series of "corrective procedures" were typed on his reports, with no elaboration of what those procedures were.

"What are these 'corrective procedures?'" Valerie asked.

"I think it best if I show you," Chester replied.

They were soon walking down a corridor that seemed seldom used. Rows of doors shut in a part of the building kept away from the children. No dorms. No recreation rooms. No classrooms.

Valerie was reminded of the disused parts of Bristlewood Orphanage and what they had been hiding. That same deep sense of foreboding returned. *What stories can you tell?* she thought. If only the walls could speak.

Chester pulled out a large nest of keys and looked for the right one. He then unlocked the door, which had a keep out sign unceremoniously hanging from it at a wonky angle.

"Where are we going?" Charlie asked as they now descended an old staircase.

"It's best I show you," was all Chester would say.

CHAPTER SEVENTEEN

Valerie could feel the air getting damper as they headed underground, and the sense of confinement that the Stevenson Reform School provided was palpably growing as they descended.

Chester led the way into the depths of the building.

"It's in here," he said, stopping at a door where the black markings left by water showed on the floor.

"Is this where you had the flood?" asked Valerie.

"The entire basement was flooded for a while; we were nearly shut down, again, for it," replied Chester. "There's an underground stream nearby, apparently, and when it floods, the basement is overwhelmed. Honestly, I'd love us to move to another building, but there's no funding for that."

The door opened, and Chester showed everyone a corridor with dripping walls and seven iron doors along them. The walls were covered in dark patches of mold against discolored white tiles, and the doors themselves were red with rust.

"I hate coming in here. To think what they did..." Chester trailed off.

Valerie stepped forward and touched one of the rusted iron doors. It felt like ice to the touch.

"These doors... They're prison cells?"

Chester wore a troubled look upon his shoulders.

"I don't want to say anything that I'm not sure of," he said, "but I believe each of these is, in effect, a cell. The doors lock with a keyhole on the outside only and each of them has a small slit that looks like it was for food to be pushed through."

Valerie was struck with a feeling of nausea. It was as if she could breathe in the history of the place. All the pain. All the torment. All the injustice.

What disgusted Valerie the most was that, at one time, practices like that were normal. This was what it once meant to take care of troubled children. But to think that secretly, such places were still being used within recent decades, that was the most shocking thing of all.

"What was going on here?" Will asked, his voice filled with confusion, as if he were trying to reconcile the horrible environment with his own ideals of professional child care. "Wasn't this shut down?"

"My predecessors," Chester said, "they had almost Victorian ideas about treating violent children. This was their little secret. Where they could deal with the worst behaviors in the school. All away from visitors and inspectors. Out of sight, out of mind."

Chester opened the door, its rusted hinges squeaked unnaturally. Inside, a small room with crumbling plaster walls and no windows lay in shadows.

"What was done in here?" Valerie asked.

"This is the... The 'corrective' room. It was originally set up to help the children, but I think you can guess what they used it for." For a moment, Chester's voice cracked slightly.

Valerie was taken with that. This was a man who had genuine remorse for things people had done in that building years before he arrived.

"What you're seeing here," Chester said, pulling down a light switch, "is the entire legacy of the Stevenson Reform School. The ultimate failure of the system to change the lives of our most troubled children."

The lights flickered on, and before them the stark damp walls held shadows cast from a single bed frame and an old bucket.

"Blake Harlow was one of the worst behaved kids to come in here, and that's saying something because a lot of them were extremely disturbed and violent. He was pretty much a psychopath right from the start, and his record shows it," said Chester. "But no one, never mind a child, deserves to have their humanity robbed like this."

"What do you mean by that?" Valerie asked.

"As soon as Blake came here, he was showing signs of sociopathy and psychopathy. He was practically just out of diapers, and he'd already put a knife to his baby brother's throat."

Valerie raised her eyebrows. She was intrigued and unnerved by her thoughts. Was a killer like Blake Harlow made by his environment? Or was he innately evil? Would even a good person leave a place like that without carrying violence, anger, and resentment in their heart? Either way, he hadn't had much chance to find a better path in life.

"And they locked the children in here?" she asked.

"Yes, Agent Law," said Chester. "This was the 'corrective procedure' that teachers used here for years. There's another term for

99

it."

"Solitary confinement," answered Charlie.

Chester nodded.

"Solitary confinement has such a harmful impact on a person's well-being," Will offered. "But children can't understand long term consequences and what misery and torment comes with being removed from all human contact. Even with such a horrendous punishment, I doubt a young Blake Harlow or anyone else could have fully comprehended they'd end up here for any misbehavior."

"And there were many of them," Chester said. "Just look at the file."

Valerie opened the folder in her hands once more. Chester was right. Each page was filled with a short description of some misdemeanor, followed by the cryptic words of 'corrective procedure carried out.'

Blake punched a student: Corrective procedure carried out for 5 days.

Blake stole food from the cafeteria: Corrective procedure carried out for 3 days.

Blake tried to run away: Corrective procedure carried out for 14 days.

"Fourteen days...," Valerie said almost with a gasp. "Fourteen days in solitary confinement at just 13 years of age. I can't imagine the sort of damage..."

"And look," said Will, peering over Valerie's shoulder at the file. "How many times was he in solitary confinement?"

"More than any other student I've heard of," answered Chester. "What sort of damage does being locked up in a room by yourself for so long do to a fragile young mind?"

Valerie handed the folder to Will and stepped towards the old bed frame.

"My God," she said, noticing something on the wall.

"What is it?" asked Charlie.

Valerie ran her hand over the wall, her fingers dipping into two deep, inch-wide holes in the plaster.

"Charlie, do you remember the Tully case?" Valerie asked.

Charlie moved over to the wall and inspected the holes himself.

"You're right," he said with a deep sigh. "These look the same."

"The Tully Case?" Chester asked. "I'm afraid I don't know what you're referring to."

Charlie turned to Chester.

"It was a famous abduction case back in the '80s. Paul Tully had kidnapped several young boys and held them in his basement for months." Charlie wiped his brow, the atmosphere of the place seemingly weighing down on him. "A tip off led some cops to one of his neighbor's homes. They got the wrong house. Tully saw this and knew he was close to being found out."

"I remember this case!" Will said with far too much enthusiasm. "Because of the botched raid it gave Tully time to... dispose of the boys."

"My word," Chester said. "This is all a little too much for me."

"He killed the boys," Valerie said, her voice grim. "Then he tried to clean up. And he nearly got away with it, as well. By the time the cops realized their mistake and searched Tully's house, the bodies were gone and the basement, where he'd kept them alive for a while, looked like any normal basement."

"Except for the holes in the wall," Charlie explained. "One of the investigating cops realized that a few small holes in the plaster of the basement were evidence of something unthinkable. They had once had bolts stuck in them."

"I don't understand what that has to do with this here?" Chester inquired

"These holes are the same as in the Tully case," Valerie said. "Blake Harlow wasn't just confined to the room down here; he was chained to the wall like an animal."

"That's awful," Chester said. "To think with all the good we're now doing here, that something so heinous occurred down here."

"Mr. Quill, thank you for this," Valerie said, pointing to the folder in Will's hand. "We're also anticipating significant escalation on Blake Harlow's part. It's imperative to have some officers stand guard inside the school, and at every entrance and fire exit. I know it's not ideal, but we're dealing with a bloodthirsty killer, and I refuse to take any more chances."

Chester turned sheet white.

"Of course... You don't think he'll come here, do you?"

"He seems to be visiting his old haunts," Charlie answered. "And settling old grudges. Do you know if there's anyone still working here from that time?"

"There's no one," Chester answered. "We changed all the staff after the scandal; even the cleaners are different."

"Let's hope he knows that," Valerie said. "Hopefully he'd avoid coming here in that case, if he is truly hunting down people who have crossed him."

Chester nodded, his face filled with anxiety.

"You'll be well protected here," Charlie said reassuringly. "But Mr. Quill, it would be helpful to have the names and addresses of everyone who worked here at that time. We can then see if any of them are still in the area and possible targets."

"I'll make sure your office receives all of that as quickly as possible. It might take a few hours, though. As you can see, our record keeping is a bit haphazard."

Valerie looked around at the cramped, damp room, and wondered.

"How many kids were broken down here?" she said, almost to herself.

"He's not a kid anymore," Charlie said with a grave expression. "He's a killer, and we can't lose sight of that. We need to come up with a better game plan to catch him. Come on."

Charlie moved to the stairs and the others followed. Valerie could feel the malevolence of the room behind them as they walked.

None of them looked back.

CHAPTER EIGHTEEN

Valerie felt the cold gravel writhe and crack beneath her feet. Standing still for a moment, she closed her eyes and breathed. When she didn't have to look at the Stevenson Reform School, she didn't have to think about the abuse Blake Harlow had suffered there. And how that suffering might have turned him into a killer.

"I thought we were beyond this," Will said. "Between Bristlewood Orphanage and here, it's no wonder Blake was so fractured as a child."

"He still has a choice," Charlie said. "Don't you think?"

Valerie didn't reply. She was still standing beneath the gray clouds, her eyes closed and breathing deeply through her nose. For a moment, she tried to persuade herself about the good institutions do, about how they help people. Then she saw a flash of her mother in a straightjacket in a padded cell, in her mind, and opened her eyes to avoid it.

Her personal pain was so great, she'd rather face the impersonal pain of the Stevenson Reform School and how it had locked up so many kids.

"Valerie? You okay?" Charlie asked.

She nodded.

"Charlie's right, Will," she said. "We can't forget that Blake Harlow is a ruthless killer. Most people who suffer abuse don't become abusers."

"But they are much more likely to abuse," Will replied. "Statistically speaking."

"You heard Chester in there," Charlie offered. "Even before he went to the orphanage and then here, Harlow was already twisted."

"I think it's clear," Will said, clearing his throat. "Regardless of how Blake Harlow became what he is, we have to assume that he's on a path of vengeance. He wants to wipe out everyone who ever did him wrong."

Valerie turned to look at the gray, stagnant angles of the Stevenson Reform School.

"He'll have a long list," she said quietly. "But I disagree. There's more to him, can't you feel that? The boy at the orphanage said he

103

seemed scared, almost like a child himself."

"Children are quite capable of killing, Val," said Charlie. "You know this."

Valerie turned from the building and looked at her partner.

"Maybe they are, but I don't know. He seems too fractured, too broken to do anything as systematic as kill a long list of people he hates. He's too erratic for it. He'd need to be more stable to think that clearly."

"And what do you base your opinion on that he's too unstable for logic?" Will seemed equally curious and resistant to the idea.

"Look," said Valerie. "Yes, Harlow killed the guards at the Culver Institute, paying specific attention to the one he didn't like."

"And he ended up at Bristlewood Orphanage, suggesting he was going to take out his revenge on Miss Armstrong," Will contended.

"Ah, but check this out." Valerie pulled out her cellphone and momentarily scanned through it. She then showed a picture of the local area around the Culver Institute.

"Look at the surrounding area here," she said pointing to the screen. "At the rear of the institute are some large fields and then a golf course. Beyond that a few country roads and then..."

"Bristlewood Orphanage," Charlie said.

"It wouldn't have made sense," Valerie continued, "for Blake to escape in any other direction."

"Precisely," Will said looking at the screen. "That implies that he is logical. He chose the route he'd be least likely seen."

"Maybe," Valerie added. "But think about his solitary confinement here. We know that type of treatment can lead patients to become..."

"Agoraphobic," interjected Charlie. "So, you think he might have taken the scenic route because he'd be afraid of people?" The two agents had spent so much time together on cases, it was sometimes as though they could read each other's minds.

"Yes," smiled Valerie. "Then, where does he go as night falls? The Orphanage, the only place he knows."

"I disagree, Valerie." Will scratched his cheek in thought. "He kills the guards, brutally disfiguring the one who was an authority figure to him. Then, he heads straight to the orphanage to kill Miss Armstrong. He might even have planned this all out from his cell at the Culver Institute, dreaming of killing those who have wronged him. Now he has the taste of revenge. He'll be out heading towards someone else he hates."

Valerie thought for a moment. Will's theory didn't feel right anymore. How could he be so sure that Blake Harlow was so calculating? It was an assumption, and one that no longer sat well with Valerie.

"What if killing Miss Armstrong was just a crime of opportunity?" Valerie said. "He ends up in the orphanage and then he stumbles across the horrible old woman who made his life hell? For all he would have known, she didn't even work there anymore. I don't think he's out for revenge. If he does visit any old haunts, I don't think he'll be there to kill, at least not primarily. He kills impulsively. All that anger coming out uncontrolled at once."

"There's a clear pattern of behavior here," Will said. "You're overthinking this."

That comment irked Valerie. It was the same thing her mother used to say to her. The same criticism her trainers at the Academy had given her. No. She couldn't stand that idea. She had to trust her instincts. It was her technique, her job to think things through. Sometimes she felt as though she could see elements of a person's behavior too easily overlooked by others, even highly trained experts like Will.

"Will," she continued. "With all due respect, you're a rookie in the field. I appreciate your input, but agents like Charlie and me, we have to trust our instincts. It can be the difference between someone being saved, and someone ending up with a knife in their throat from an unhinged fugitive."

Valerie turned to Charlie, but she saw something she was unaccustomed to in his eyes: Doubt.

There was an uncomfortable silence. Valerie felt so disappointed. She tried not to show it, but she could never truly hide her feelings from her partner.

"Well go on, Charlie," she said, aggravated. "Spit it out then."

"Val," Charlie said softly. "Yeah, we use our instincts, but we don't ignore the facts. And the facts are that he's already killed more than once out of revenge. We know he killed his adopted mother as well and going by what we now know about his time at this reform school, it was probably out of revenge for sending him here in the first place."

"Ah," said Val, her index finger pointing to the bleak sky, "but the mother was the one who didn't want him sent there. Remember? It was the father who persuaded her to make him go."

"It's likely," Will interjected, "that Blake didn't know that. The parents probably presented a unified front, even though the mother was reluctant. Charlie is right, and insightful here. That was another case of revenge. It's turning into Blake Harlow's Modus Operandi."

"I think he'll go after the father next," Charlie said, gravely. "And now it's a two for one deal. The brother is there, too."

Valerie shook her head in disagreement.

"I disagree, Charlie," said Will. "Have you heard of chain of motive before?"

Charlie shrugged.

"It means," Will explained, too readily, "that each crime informs the next. Yes, Blake Harlow is out for revenge. It's clearly in his blood. But he's just killed the headmistress of his orphanage. That will spur him onto killing a similar target. Like someone either here at the reform school or attached to it. It's like a psychological traveling itch; had he killed a family member first after his escape, maybe then he would have targeted another person in his family. But for now, he'll be consumed by thoughts of revenge against those who were supposed to care for him in educational settings and didn't."

"We'll need to agree to disagree," Charlie said. "I think he'll head to the father's house to finish what he started decades ago."

Valerie sighed. A doubt was creeping into her heart. Listening to her two colleagues disagree with her and then each other... She wondered if the new unit wasn't just getting in its own way. Why wouldn't they listen to her?

She knew you couldn't always have everyone on the same page, but when time was against you, pulling in different directions only served to slow the chase.

Will's phone let out a loud ping. He pulled the phone out of his pocket and read the message. Looking up, he had an uncomfortable look on his face.

Valerie crossed her arms in disapproval.

"You've got to be joking, Will. Now? Again?"

"I... I'm sorry, but one of my patients needs me," he said, putting the phone back in his pocket. "I'll meet up with you both as quickly as I can."

"I know you're trying to do what's best for your patient," said Valerie, "But time isn't a luxury we have, and Blake Harlow's next victim won't have it either."

Valerie felt bad telling it as it was, but the stakes were high. She desperately wanted the team to stay on it until the end. But she knew it was impossible.

Will said nothing. He just frowned slightly as though he didn't know what to say.

"Steady, Val," Charlie said, again softly. "It looks like we've reached a bit of a dead end here, anyway."

Valerie always knew that cases could warp things. It amazed her how quickly the tables had turned. The last time Will had to leave, it was she who was defending him.

Maybe I need a break, too, she thought, now seeing how the stress was changing her behavior.

"I'm sorry, Will," she sighed. "I just need to find him. You know? He's out there somewhere, and it's getting under my skin."

"I understand," offered Will. "I'll be back as quickly as I can."

"I'll drive you, if you want, Will," said Charlie.

"That's very kind of you, but I think I'll get a cab. It's probably in the wrong direction for you."

Valerie looked at the reform school and then walked out through the gates. They should knock that place down and put salt on the ground, she thought. Nothing good can come of it. A flash of her mother intruded in her mind. She was sitting in the same sort of room as they'd found under the floors of the reform school.

It's just tiredness, she thought to herself, shaking the image from her mind.

How she wished she could have done something about the cold, padded place where her mother now lived. But too much water had gone under the bridge. She was dangerous. She had to be kept from society.

Valerie refused to be burdened by that same old insidious familial guilt. But it still lurked underneath.

Instead, she turned her thoughts back to the case as she walked to the car. Blake Harlow was out there, and she hoped that Will, Charlie, and she could pull together to find him.

If not, she knew she'd have to call her boss, Jackson Weller, and ask for a new team.

CHAPTER NINETEEN

Harlow's mind was ramping up with violent thoughts as he sneaked down a lane between two rows of houses.

It was easy for him to slip into that mode like a pair of comfortable old shoes. Some would call it another person, another mind, another personality. But for Harlow, it was both enemy and friend at the same time.

This groove of thinking would guide him, make him think terrible thoughts. Make him salivate at the very thought of cutting flesh with steel or wrapping his hands around a victim's throat while watching their eyes bulge.

He would be the last thing they would see, and he would be smiling.

Moving to the end of the lane, the last house on the corner came into view. The house looked warm and inviting. The thought of snuffing out that comfort for someone aroused him. There was no better feeling than invading someone's world, a shadow in the night, blade in hand ready to strike like a cobra.

The two-story Victorian home with its red brick and white trim sat tucked away behind a row of trees. It was picturesque, but Harlow knew a great evil lay inside of it. And he would obliterate it with an evil of his very own making.

She was in there; he knew it. Elmira Phillips. And he would make her pay for her crimes. There were no double standards in Harlow's mind. Yes, he was violent, a brutal killer, but she had made him that way, or rather her choices had. And now she would have to come face-to-face with the product of those choices.

Killing Elmira Phillips was the one thing he could do right. He needed to do *something* right. It was his own twisted gift to himself and the world.

Breathing in and out with greater force, he could feel himself become more aroused at the thought of gutting her like a fish. He started to stroke his face for just a moment, then pushed his own hand away. He didn't want to get too emotionally involved. Not yet. Not before the denouement.

Killing was cathartic, but when the emotion took over, he could be careless. It was his precision that had kept him safer than he otherwise would have been.

But what if the *other* took over? The child. What if it took over again? Harlow was frightened of that, of losing himself to it. He wanted to have all his faculties present when making decisions and, more importantly, killing. Then it could be savored without fear of getting caught. He had waited so long for all of this, his true self hiding in the shadows biding its time. The thought of it being undermined by another psychotic shift was unbearable to him.

Allowing himself just one more indulgent thought before moving, he leaned against the side of the house and smiled, thinking about the moment he would have when he finally crossed the line at last, wiping her dirty body from the face of the earth.

Harlow had killed before, but this murder was a lifetime in the making. Perhaps when he was done, he would be free of it all.

He saw the police as bumbling fools. But what if they got lucky? His timeline would then be off. Should he move faster than planned?

If they did get lucky…

Then he would have to get away from that place, get away from the past, get away from everything. His plans would be ruined. If he were ever caught, the authorities might think him an animal. But if it came to that, an animal could live out there in the wilderness, fend for itself, and kill anyone unlucky enough to cross its path.

He held on for a world where he could walk down a street and not have to worry about being recognized by someone who had seen his face in the paper, or on the news. If detected, that would be impossible, and so retiring to the forests and mountains one day would provide good hunting grounds, should the police pursue him after.

He didn't know if the desire to kill would disappear forever after he'd finally killed her; in one way he hoped it would, but in another, he hoped it stayed. The need to cut, torture, and tear, was who he was deep down. Without it, perhaps he would be lost.

But the consequences would take care of themselves. First, he had to do this one thing right.

And Elmira would pay. Dear Elmira. Dear old lady. Dear Mother.

Harlow was content. He was happy. He was in a good mood. His time had come.

In fact, he was looking forward to this. Finally, she would reap her reward for abandoning him. He would savor this kill more than any, just as long as he could stop the child personality from stepping forward and taking over. That confused wretch who was no good to anyone. He despised it.

Stay in control and the kill will be twice as sweet, he thought.

Not yet, not yet, not yet, he said over and over to himself. He wanted the old witch to suffer. She'd know already about the escape from the Culver Institute. She would have read about the murders. She'd know her son's name.

Maybe I'll let her quake in fear for one more day. One more day until she finally gets what's coming to her.

The thought of manipulating everything to his desired schedule thrilled him.

As he walked back away from the house, he was already settled on how he'd kill her when he returned. As long as the child could be kept at bay.

CHAPTER TWENTY

Valerie stared at the phone in her hand. She sat alone on the couch in her apartment. She was alone because she wanted no one, not even her boyfriend to hear.

He'd offered to see her that night. But he knew nothing of her mother, of her secret. This was something she had to face alone.

What would he think of her if he knew the truth? That she'd practically abandoned her own mother to a high-security psychiatric ward? Valerie herself didn't know what to make of it, so what chance did anyone else have of understanding?

The phone had been sitting there in her left palm for nearly an hour. The other hand was doing its best to lubricate the stress of it all, one glass of red wine at a time. Alcohol was a professional hazard in her line of work. She'd seen several good agents, even some great ones, become dependent on alcohol to cope with the stress. All it took was a push in the wrong direction, sip by sip. A family crisis was enough to push any anxious agent over the precipice.

She wasn't quite there yet. Valerie had managed to hold her life together. But she knew the danger of relying on alcohol to soothe her pain: a poor master and a poor servant. And yet, there she was, still drinking that night.

Glance at the phone.

Remember the pain.

Drink to forget.

But Valerie couldn't forget. Not the memories of her childhood with her sister and mom, and not professionally after the last couple of days. Tracking Blake Harlow was the most important case of her career, and she felt like she was failing. The last thing she needed was for there to be new issues about her mom's care.

And then there was the worry about her team. Everything felt like it was moving in the wrong direction. A runaway train too far gone to call back.

She felt that Charlie and Will were wrong, but she couldn't quite put her finger on the map. Where to next, Val? Where will Blake

Harlow strike next? It was a mystery.

Police were watching Harlow's adopted father's house, and they had a bulkier presence at the Stevenson Reform School now. But he hadn't been seen. He was a ghost moving in the shadows.

Valerie closed her eyes and took a deep breath.

"Forget," she said on the exhale.

She'd been taught at the Academy to decouple from a case once home. This was how you avoided getting too deep and too burned up. This was how you avoided *needing* to have a glass of wine to sleep.

"Remember that your work shouldn't follow you home," one of her old tutors at the academy had said.

But Valerie had never been able to do that. Her cases coursed through her veins. This one more than most. People's lives were on the line. This wasn't an office job of sending emails and chatting idly at the water cooler about the latest episode of a mediocre TV show.

Valerie's job mattered. It was life and death to the victims and their families. Right or wrong, Valerie felt that it should be life and death to her as well.

Staring across the coffee table to the cream wall above her fireplace, Valerie looked at the blankness of it. A daze fell over her. Images, thoughts, raced through her mind: Blake Harlow, a child chained to a bed, no daylight, a bucket for a toilet, isolated and removed from even a glint of happiness.

Then the image of Blake morphed into another. It was her mom sitting on that rusted bed frame, her hair and eyes wild, tears streaming down her face and all along wondering where her daughter Valerie had gone and why she didn't visit.

Valerie, where are you...

What did I do wrong...

Shouldn't a daughter look after their sick mother...

A tear rolled down Valerie's cheek. It dripped down onto the back of her hand. She turned the hand upward. Her phone was still there. It was still ready to dial that forgotten number.

Downing the last of the red wine in her glass, Valerie finally hit the call button.

The phone rang several times; each time she thought about hanging up. Deep down, she hoped no one answered. When she heard the click of the call beginning, her stomach sank, feeling like a bottomless pit of dread and regret.

"Where the hell have you been?" the voice of Valerie's sister yelled.

"I'm... I'm sorry... It's been a tough few days," was all Valerie could say.

"You've been constantly ignoring my messages and calls; don't you care about Mom?"

"I do... I just..."

"Get your priorities straight, Valerie," the voice on the phone said. "We need you."

There was a silence. Valerie wanted to say sorry again, but she knew that actions speak louder than words. The truth was, deep down in that nest of family stress at the bottom of her stomach, she didn't want to see her mother. She never had. Not with their past.

There's no future for us... she thought. *Not a meaningful one.*

"How is she?" Valerie finally asked.

"Not good," came the reply. "She's deteriorating. And despite me being the one who visits her, she keeps asking for you."

Valerie's heart felt like it dropped from her chest. "Mom keeps asking for me?" she asked with a slight tremor to her voice.

"She's delusional. Or maybe she's just trying to make amends."

"Or make me feel guilty. Trick me into visiting so she can go off again."

"The guilt works though, huh?"

"I know," Valerie said. "I just... I can't... I can't do this right now."

"You can't see her because you're too damn scared... because you're weak," the voice said. "Big shot FBI agent, and you can't face up to what happened."

Valerie felt the color draining from her face. She was in no condition to go over the past, never mind the future. Calling had been a bad idea. At least her mother was alive, and that was good enough for now.

"I've got to go," she said.

"Running away, again?" Valerie's sister said. "And leaving me holding it all together. As usual. Well, you just go off with your fancy badge and your detective work; go off sorting out other people's problems. Never mind your little sister's!"

"I... I'm sorry. I'll phone in the next couple of days," she said, finally hitting the end call button on the phone, fast enough to cut off her sister from saying anything else that might sting.

She set the phone down on the glass table. Her sister thought she was weak, but that couldn't be, could it? Valerie had done everything to push and test herself over the years. But there was that one glaring omission: her mother and her treatment. That one fight she could never bring herself to have.

Not after what her mother did.

"I'm not weak," she muttered to herself.

Valerie poured another glass of wine, but instead of drinking it, she put it on the table and then sobbed into her hands. She was so torn over her mother. The abuse. The fear she'd subjected Valerie to as a girl.

But then there was the tenderness. The random acts of kindness. The stories at bedtime and the warm hugs whenever something went wrong.

That was before the breakdown. Before the psychosis. Before the knife.

Valerie's phone sprung into life. It was her boyfriend. She didn't have the energy to pretend things were okay. And she didn't have the energy to open her heart to him either.

She just stared at the phone and watched it ring, and ring, and ring, before silence fell.

"You're running away from everything again," Valerie said out loud. "And talking to yourself is a sure sign you're losing your mind."

Yes, Valerie. That's your fear, isn't it. That you're like your mother. That the illness is there. The compulsion to hurt. To maim. Even to kill. That's why you're good at your job. That's why you can get inside their heads. Because you know the truth behind it all: You're one of them.

"It's the drink talking," Valerie said, defiantly. "It's the drink talking." The second time didn't sound as certain.

The phone rang again. Valerie picked it up to throw it across the room, but instead she read a different name on the caller ID. It was Jackson Weller.

She could run away from everything. But her work, her cases, her need to find Blake Harlow and put him away, that was something she would always run towards. It was all she could live for right now.

"Agent Law?"

"Yes, Boss."

"I just read your email. Some interesting insights, but it looks like you've hit a dead end," Jackson said.

"I'm working on some things... Some threads...," Valerie tried her best to pull herself together. "We'll be back at HQ tomorrow."

As if Jackson could sense the nerves in her voice, he asked: "Are you okay, Agent Law? You sound a little off?"

"Yes, I'm on it, Sir. I'm on it."

Silence for a moment, as if Jackson was considering his next move carefully.

"I'm not wanting to stress you further, but between the killing of Miss Armstrong and the fact that Blake Harlow managed to escape from a high-security facility, I'm getting more pressure from up top. He needs to be in custody. Now."

"I... I know, Sir. We'll regroup in the morning and double our efforts."

"I hope so, Agent Law. For your benefit and mine. Keep me updated and remember to use Will Cooper as much as possible. He's a goldmine."

Valerie wanted to hang up again. Was this Jackson's way of telling her he had little faith in her findings?

"I'll certainly consult with him."

"Make sure that you do. Now, go get some rest. The media are having a field day over this, and every minute wasted is another bad headline."

"Of course, Sir." Valerie felt some of the wine coming back up her throat. She managed to keep it down, but the acidity burned inside.

"And Agent Law... Valerie... If this is too much for you," Jackson said with a softer tone. "I can have you moved to another department. It needn't hurt your career."

"I'll be fine," Valerie said. But even she was unsure of those words. "Goodnight."

The call ended, and Valerie curled up on her couch. She hoped she wouldn't have any more nightmares, but she knew she would. As she fell asleep, she saw flashes of Blake Harlow's face in her mind, grinning, wide-eyed, taunting, and drenched in blood.

"I'll get you tomorrow," Valerie said quietly. Then the apartment fell into silence, as she knew the only place that she could now seek answers was back in the case room of the Mesmer building. There must have been something they'd overlooked.

CHAPTER TWENTY ONE

Valerie studied the notes and photographs on the case wall, trying her best to block out the noise coming from the next room.

Charlie was in there, trying his best to explain to Jackson Weller why they were back at the Mesmer building rather than out looking for the killer. He could hear the muffled words. Charlie was defending Valerie's decisions to the hilt. Whether this was his usual loyalty or that he had come around to her way of thinking about the case, she didn't know yet.

Valerie pinned a picture of the reform school to the case board and the orphanage next to it. She stood back to take them in.

"Where are you, Blake Harlow," she said under her breath, "and where will you go next?"

The noise and smell of black coffee being poured entered Valerie's mind.

She was still too focused on figuring out Blake Harlow's next move to notice Will Cooper standing next to her holding out a hot mug of coffee.

"Oh," she said. "You're back. Thanks." She took the cup and the strong smell helped wake her still groggy mind.

"I am back, yes," Will said, pushing his glasses up his nose. "I'm sorry if I gave the impression yesterday that I wanted to leave you in the lurch."

"We were all a little frayed yesterday, Will," Valerie said, taking a sip of the coffee. She frowned. "I think that coffee machine has seen better days."

Will laughed.

"Yes, but then do we really drink it for the taste or are we just looking for the drug?"

Will stared for a moment at Valerie. She noticed him. She noticed that nervous stare.

"Is something on your mind, Will?"

"I... I was up half the night thinking about the case."

"Well, that's good. At least I wasn't the only one."

"I'm wondering if I've bitten off more than I can chew with this field work, Valerie," Will said, far more bashfully than he had ever seemed before. "You see, the academic work is simple. I study the words, the case files, even interview criminals from time to time. But they're already caught. This is different. Lives are on the line. I hate to feel that I'm not contributing enough to you and Charlie, or even putting you on the wrong track."

Valerie looked into Will's wise gaze and saw something she hadn't noticed before. A frailty. It seemed to her that their disagreement over Blake's next move had taken the wind out of his sails. He was doubting himself.

"Will, you're talented," Valerie said, calmly. "You've already given us a lot of insight, and I'm glad you're part of the team. Even if we disagree sometimes." She let out a smirk.

Will laughed, but then looked back down at his own cup of coffee.

"Do you ever feel out of your depth when chasing people? Like the stress of it... If you don't catch the perp soon, there'll be another death..."

"All the time, Will. All the time. But you can't beat yourself up. Investigators make mistakes. They hit dead ends. We just have to pull back and think through what we know again."

Valerie looked across the room and through the glass wall. She could see Charlie being animated with Jackson and Jackson being animated with him.

Finally, Jackson threw up his hands in frustration and walked out of the corridor and to somewhere else less stressful. Charlie shrugged and smiled at Valerie and Will through the glass before entering the room.

"He's not a happy man," Charlie said.

"Let me guess," said Valerie. "He's wondering why we're here and not out there looking for Harlow?"

"Yup," Charlie said. "I just said you were right to come back here. I didn't tell him how persuasive you were on the phone this morning." He hesitated for a moment. "Val... Are you sure about this? We could at least be sitting nearby Blake Harlow's father's house or the reform school. We might get lucky."

"Charlie," Valerie said with a knowing smile. "We've been through a lot, but I'm asking you and Will to trust me on this. Blake Harlow isn't going to go looking for his dad, at least not yet. We're missing a piece of the puzzle trying to figure out his next move."

"I'd suggest getting more into Blake Harlow's head," Will offered.

"But it sounds as if you've already been in there quite a bit."

Valerie knew this was a joke, but it hit a nerve. That old worry, the worry of being too easily able to think a killer's thoughts, to anticipate their moves, it led to a frightening place. What if one day she got so deep into the muck of a sadistic killer's personality, that she couldn't get out? Would she become just like them?

She stepped back from the case board, its surface littered with pinned notes and images of the case, and then took another deep breath.

"You're not really going to...," Charlie said.

"Hold on Charlie," said Will. "I've seen this technique before, imagining the world from the killer's perspective. With the right person, the right imagination and insight, they can glean their behavioral patterns and come up with new leads."

Charlie turned and looked at his partner, respect in his eyes. But there was worry there, too. Valerie glanced back at him. *Does he know?* she thought. *Does he know how much doing this stuff hurts me?*

She plastered a smile on her face and then returned her gaze to the board.

"I remember Dr. Hoffman's class at the academy," she said.

"Laurence Hoffman?" Will asked. "He was one of a kind. I'm sorry he passed."

"So was I," Valerie said somberly. "He gave a talk once on his immersion technique. It's similar to what you mentioned, Will. Trying to burn away your own perspective to see through the eyes of the killer... I know you're skeptical, Charlie."

"Hey, Val. Whatever works. I just think we shouldn't abandon good old fashioned detective work either."

"Of course! But there's something to this technique," Valerie said, still staring at the case board "It's a little like schizophrenia," she said. "You try to inhabit the killer's mind, to feel what they feel and think what they think. A madness, but one that's carefully controlled. Too many thoughts go in, and the mind becomes unstable. I saw Professor Hoffman do it once... he almost went into a catatonic state."

"I've heard of his immersion technique, but never actually seen it firsthand," said Will.

"I've tried it before, mainly in my own time," Valerie said.

"You're own time?" Charlie asked sounding worried.

Valerie nodded.

"You sit in a bar, and you see someone who is overly aggressive. You observe their movements, their body language. Maybe you sit near

118

enough to them to eavesdrop on their conversation. But that's not enough to think like them. You need something else. One more ingredient."

"A hook?" Will suggested. "I've heard some of these techniques require that, but I'm not too familiar with the specifics."

"That's right, Will," Valerie said. "You need a hook. So you listen in at the bar, listening to what the man is talking about. Finally, you find it. A hook. Something that creates movement in his life. He mentions his father has recently passed and he lost his job the week before.

"Now you have something to hold onto. You combine his movements; you feel them in yourself. You build a profile in your head of how he feels about the world. Lost. Angry. Insecure. You predict that he'll start a fight with someone soon enough. And, of course, he does."

"It sounds like profiling but from the inside out," Charlie said.

"You always know how to break it down into its core concept, Charlie. That's exactly what it is."

Valerie wanted to share the cost of it all. The pain thinking like a criminal, a violent one, could bring. It was one thing to predict a drunk's behavior at a bar, but quite another to think like a sadistic killer.

"So, try it," Charlie said. "You need a hook, right?"

"That's what I've been wracking my brains for," she said. "But I can't think of the right one. It needs to be something that causes direction in Blake Harlow's life. And not just that, but something that will move him in a direction, right now."

"Val," Charlie said. "I believe in you. If you think this immersion trick is going to work. Then I think you should go for it."

"Thanks, Charlie," Valerie replied. "I know the three of us have the talents to catch Harlow. We just need a push in the right direction. I've been staring at these photographs on the case board. The reform school. Harlow's dad's home. But neither of them fit; I can feel it."

"Then maybe your hook is another place, Val. Where else would he go, and why?"

Valerie looked at the photographs on the board and then closed her eyes. She breathed deeply and began searching.

A hook.

A hook.

A hook.

There had to be something that would motivate Blake Harlow

beyond revenge. Valerie saw in her mind the halls of Bristlewood Orphanage. She saw Miss Armstrong responding to a sound in a room, and then entering, only to be killed. But there was more to it... There was more...

Yes, the room was where Harlow had slept as a boy. But why? Was it truly just revenge?

Then Valerie's mind instinctively went deeper. She saw Blake Harlow as a child in the dorm room. Yes, the place was a terror. Yes, he was mistreated. But as Valerie played out Blake's experiences in her mind, she felt something else in that room.

Comfort.

When the overbearing teachers were asleep, when the other boys stopped their taunts, in the silence of the night, a comfort came to Blake Harlow. Curled up in his bed under the blankets, feeling warm, protected, away from all the hurt. Those wee small hours were precious, because they were the only time when the pain stopped.

Valerie opened her eyes. She looked at the board again and let out an excited gasp.

"Did you get something?" Will asked.

"A hook, Val?"

"Look at this." Valerie stepped forward and pulled at some notes on the board. "All of Blake Harlow's victims died at night. Maybe... Maybe it's because that was the only pleasurable time in his life. A time at the orphanage and the reform school where he'd be left alone to himself, to his thoughts.

"In that confinement even at the reform school. He must have laid there at night when they turned out the lights. That could have become a place where he felt strongest, in a bizarre way. And maybe even a dissociative personality could have developed. A friend he could talk to, a constant companion, like a coping mechanism. Remember the kid at the orphanage said he heard Blake Harlow talking to himself."

"Yes, that's right!" Will interjected. "This would make sense. It would explain why his actions are sometimes instinctive and unpredictable, and other times calculating. When exactly such a hypothetical switch occurs, though, we couldn't be sure."

"If nighttime and comfort are the places where he's drawn to," Charlie stated. "Then, is that why he went to the orphanage and his old room? To experience that old feeling of comfort in his bed? Then Miss Armstrong happened in on him? Maybe she had no time to react, not because he was waiting for her, but because he was lying in darkness and she just couldn't see him."

"It's a theory," Will said. "But we'd need more to go on. How does this hook of nocturnal comfort help us find him?"

"Because," Valerie said, turning to her colleagues with a smile. "He's not out for revenge right now, he's looking for that comfort. And he can only get that in one place. The original home where he and his brother were adopted. The place where he was able to be normal for a time, and where he then killed his adopted mother."

"It's worth a try," Will said. "I just hope we're not too late. He might have already been and gone by now."

Valerie had a sinking feeling in her stomach. Will was right. Perhaps Blake Harlow had already visited his old home, and if he had, what horrors had he left behind there?

CHAPTER TWENTY TWO

Helen Ramirez didn't know what lay in store for her at home. If she had, she'd never have stepped inside.

The house was on a quiet corner of a quiet street. It was an idyllic place, complete with picket fence and a play park across the road.

The perfect place to bring up children.

The perfect place to start a life.

But life has a way of twisting the knife when you least expect it.

Helen had just been to get some groceries. Her husband Fred had been laid up from work for two weeks after breaking his ankle at the warehouse. She was a little sick of his complaining all the time, not that he didn't have something to complain about this time. He did. But he was the proverbial boy who cried wolf.

Despite the annoyance, she'd decided she'd been a little too harsh on him of late. And so, she snuck out in the afternoon to grab some ingredients to make his favorite treat - cinnamon pancakes.

That trip to the store only took 26 minutes. But that was long enough for something dark and malevolent to walk into Helen and Fred's life, changing it forever.

Helen entered the yard of the old house and walked up the front steps, key in one hand, brown grocery bag in the other.

That was when she noticed that the door was already open. She could have sworn she'd closed it. And Fred could barely get up out of his chair on his crutches, so there was little chance he'd somehow sneaked out to go to O'Malley's Bar, one of his favorite haunts.

Helen pushed the door open further. It creaked on its hinges. Fred always said he'd oil them, but he never did, like a multitude of things left for another day around their home.

"Fred?" Helen said, stepping over the threshold into her home.

It had always been a homey place for Helen. A place of sanctuary. But in that moment, it felt as though a chill had entered the house. Something wasn't right. She could feel it in her bones.

"Fred?" she asked again as she walked into the kitchen and put the groceries down on the counter.

There was no answer.

Maybe he's fallen asleep, she thought to herself. *Maybe*.

Looking at the kitchen counter, something was now apparent. Her stainless-steel kitchen knives, the ones Fred had disappointingly bought her for Christmas, sat in their wooden block slots.

One knife was missing. The boning knife.

"Fred" she said again, but this time with a tremble in her throat. She moved over to the knives and grabbed one of them. Something she had never, ever, felt the need to do in her own home before.

A thumping noise sneaked through the kitchen doorway.

Helen's heart raced.

She stepped forward, telling herself it was all in her head. Fred had probably made his way to the kitchen to get the knife for something. Cutting a thread from his clothes or cutting up some of his chewing tobacco.

And what about the open front door, Helen? She still couldn't explain that.

Another thump came.

Helen walked nervously into the hallway and then finally into the living room.

What she saw made her heart stop.

There was a huge man sitting in their old armchair, facing the television and seemingly watching it.

Fred was lying on the floor on his back. He had a cut across his nose and his eyes were shut, but he was breathing.

Helen screamed.

The large man in the armchair looked up.

"Why are you in my house?" he said. "Why are you here? Where's Mom and Dad? What have you done with them!?"

"Get out of my house," Helen said, her voice trembling.

The man stood up. He towered above Helen. Stepping over Fred's unconscious body, he moved towards her.

"Please... Don't hurt me," Helen said, holding a hand in front of her. "Take whatever you want."

"I want to know what you've done with my mother and father. They live here. Why are you in their house?"

"We're the Ramirez's," Helen answered. "We've lived here for years."

The man shook his head, rubbing his brow with one hand while brandishing the knife with the other.

"No, no, no. Mark and Jessie Harlow live here... I don't understand. My brother Arthur is here, too... Dad! Mom! Arthur!"

The man yelled, but no answer came.

"Saints preserve us," Helen said, now knowing who was standing before her. She and Fred had gotten the house cheap, really cheap. That is what happens when someone has been murdered in a house. People get superstitious.

"You're...," Helen said. "You're the Harlow boy, aren't you?"

"Yes...," the man said, his eyes wide and bulging. "Where's my family?"

"They've been gone for years," Helen answered. "Don't you remember what you did?"

The man thumped the side of his head with his fist. He shook his head from side to side as if trying to shake a horrible memory from his mind.

"No!" The man moved forward towards Helen, holding the knife. But just as he did, Fred moved suddenly on the floor, grabbing hold of the man's leg. He dug his nails into the skin at the back of his left calf as far in as he could.

The man yelped, looked down and then thrust the boning knife through Fred's hand. Fred cried out in agony.

Helen turned and fled.

If only she could make it to the front door. She could get help. She could stop this madness. But the imposing man was quickly behind her, and he would not let her go so easily.

CHAPTER TWENTY THREE

Valerie held onto the dashboard for dear life as Charlie skidded the car around a corner. While Charlie had a determined look on his face as the engine revved, Will was in the back seat looking like he was about to vomit his lunch.

A row of pristine suburban houses came into view. Charlie reached the corner and slammed on the breaks. The car mounted the empty sidewalk. As soon as it came to rest, Valerie unclipped her seat belt, drew her gun and leaped out of the vehicle.

"Stay here, Will!" she shouted, running towards the last house on the street.

Charlie didn't draw his gun. Instead, he left the vehicle, leaped over a fence and pulled out his FBI ID card. He brandished it at a couple of parents playing with their kids in an idyllic play park.

"There's a killer on the loose," he said, breathing heavily. "Evacuate the area. Now!"

Blood drained from the parents' faces and they scooped up their children like a tsunami was coming, jumped into their own cars and sped off away from the danger.

Valerie looked across the road at Charlie before rushing through a garden gate. Now Charlie drew his weapon, holding it expertly, poised and ready. He ran behind Valerie.

"What's the play," he whispered.

"No time for a play," Valerie said. "We go in."

Valerie ran up a few stone steps and saw that the front door was lying open. She looked at Charlie, nervously. A look that said only one thing: He's already here.

"FBI!" Valerie commanded. "We're coming in, armed."

Valerie moved forward first, steadying her breathing to reduce any unnecessary shake in her hand.

Charlie followed, glaring along his arm and down the sights of his revolver.

Signaling with one hand silently, Valerie showed Charlie her path of exploration. She moved quickly to the edge of an open doorway and then silently entered the kitchen.

Nothing untoward. But Valerie's training came to her aid. She noticed two knives missing from the knife block.

Was one of them now in Blake Harlow's possession? Valerie imagined the other being taken for defense. She hoped the people living there had been able to fend him off.

Charlie came up behind her and leaned his head around the door.

"Clear," he whispered. Then he lifted his chin and gestured down the hallway to his partner.

Valerie and Charlie crept down the hallway towards another open doorway. This time, a noise was coming from inside. It was like a whimpering sound, momentarily broken by occasional whispered outburst.

"Not again. Not again," a sinister voice said in hushed tones.

Valerie felt her pulse raise. Was it the voice of Blake Harlow? Valerie moved and then threw open the door to the living room.

She aimed her weapon as she entered the room. The room was a blood bath.

Two butchered bodies lay on the floor. Valerie knew instinctively that they were the people who now lived at that address. On the floor were two sets of bloodied drag marks, where the bodies had been moved to each other.

Kneeling beside them, was the large and wide-eyed figure of Blake Harlow.

This is it, Valerie thought, trying to steady her nerve.

Valerie didn't say anything at first, she only noted the large kitchen knife in the man's hand, covered in dripping blood.

"Blake Harlow," Valerie said loudly. "Put the knife down and lie flat on the floor."

"No, no no," Blake said shaking his head. "I... I didn't do this."

Somewhere nearby, Valerie could hear movement. She knew it was Charlie. There was another entrance to the room at the rear.

He's looking to get the jump on Harlow, she thought.

"You killed them," Valerie said, pointing her gun at him from across the room. "We know that you did, Blake."

"No," Blake said. "It's not me. It's not me."

"It is you," Valerie said, edging forward. She now changed tact. Will and Charlie would have said that Blake's confusion was another charade.

Valerie felt different. *He's so fractured*, she thought.

126

"Do you not remember doing this?" she asked Blake Harlow as Charlie quietly emerged from the doorway behind the killer.

"I didn't do it!" the man screamed, waving the knife in front of him wildly.

Charlie nodded to Valerie as he walked silently just a few feet now behind Blake.

"The blood, Blake," Valerie said, in an almost mesmerizing tone. "You're covered in it. Your clothes are soaked. You must remember that."

Harlow shook his head.

"I don't," he said. "I don't."

Hugging the wall as he walked, Charlie stepped a little closer. Blake still hadn't noticed him, and Valerie knew Charlie would wait until the right moment to try to disarm him.

Valerie lowered her weapon slowly. She wanted to bring him in without killing him. And that meant getting too close for comfort.

"Look, my weapon is down," she said, holstering it. "I'm not here to harm you. I'm here to help you."

Blake said nothing. He only looked at her, his face smeared in blood.

Charlie stopped just out of reach.

Valerie raised her hands up in a non-threatening gesture.

"No guns, Blake. I've put mine away; can you put your knife away and we'll talk?"

"No, no, no," he said. "You'll just put me away... Stevenson... Bristlewood... Worse places..."

Valerie sensed that Blake was stuck in a psychological loop. He was living out his past.

"You'll never have to go back to the reform school or Bristlewood, Blake," Valerie said, softly. "If you just put the knife down and talk to me."

Blake looked down at the two dead bodies beside him.

"Who are these people? Why are they living in Mom and Dad's house?"

"Mom and Dad?" Valerie asked.

"Mark and Jessica Harlow," he said. "Where are my family? What have you done with them?"

The man's face turned to a snarl. An animalistic, vengeful look baying for blood. He rushed forward, far faster than Valerie had anticipated for a man so large.

The knife swung at Valerie's face.

Charlie squeezed the trigger, but like lightning, Blake turned and knocked the gun from his hand as it went off.

The bullet grazed Blake's shoulder and then hit the wall and deflected into the ceiling.

Charlie yelled in pain as Blake screamed and sliced his bicep with the knife.

Blake then turned again and swung the butt of the knife at Valerie's head. She ducked and it smashed into her neck, making her choke.

Valerie dropped to her knees and the blade came at her, this time aimed at her face. She reached up with speed and caught Blake's wrist.

He pushed down with his weight and strength, the knife dangling above her face. It was too much. She had to use his strength against him.

Falling to the side, Blake stumbled over her. As he fell, she turned his wrist and angled the blade up.

Blake let out a horrid cry as the blade punctured his shoulder.

Charlie jumped on top of him and pulled his arms back, cuffing him. Blood was gushing from the wound on Charlie's arm, running down the cuff of his jacket and down across his hands and fingers.

Valerie caught her breath.

"You okay, Charlie?"

"I think so; my arm's still working so he can't have cut right through the muscle."

Blake was breathing heavily; he'd passed out from the pain.

Charlie looked at the hilt of the knife, the entire blade having penetrated the man's shoulder.

"That was some move, Val," he said. "We've got him."

Valerie looked at the two dead bodies on the floor.

"I just wish we'd gotten here sooner," she said.

Sirens wailed outside as a patrol car arrived on the scene.

"I'll radio for an ambulance for me and our dear friend Blake, here," Charlie said, standing up and pulling the radio from his belt.

Valerie looked at Blake's unconscious, blood-soaked face. Then again at the bodies of Helen and Fred Ramirez next to him.

Blake was undoubtedly a violent and brutal killer. But Valerie felt this was born out of confusion more than anything else. That didn't excuse it. Far from it; he would have to face justice for his crimes.

"You caught, him. Fantastic work," Will said, walking behind an officer.

"Thanks, Will," Valerie said.

But as the paramedics and other police officers entered the scene to take Blake Harlow away, something still didn't sit right with her. His motivations, the deep desires that had fueled his hideous crimes. They didn't jive well with her profile.

His personality was shattered. In many instances throughout the case, he had been highly intelligent and conniving, but that confrontation had revealed someone, not just psychotic, but lost.

There was no precision to the Blake Harlow Valerie had just encountered.

The man was a puzzle, and she'd need to interview him to find the missing piece.

CHAPTER TWENTY FOUR

It was the kind of recognition Valerie should have sought as an FBI agent. But recognition meant nothing to Valerie when lives had been lost. Those losses, Blake Harlow's victims, could never be brought back.

Jackson Weller grinned from ear to ear as he entered the CPU office with handshakes for Will, Charlie, and Valerie. Bringing down a violent serial killer on the run should have been a great feeling. But for Valerie, it only filled her mind with unease.

Blake Harlow wasn't what she expected. All of her training painted him as a methodical killer; but her instincts, they said quite the opposite. It didn't make sense.

"Well done, Agent Law," Jackson said shaking her hand vigorously. "I knew you could do it. The first of many triumphs for the Criminal Psychopathy Unit."

"Thanks, Boss," Valerie said.

Charlie gave a knowing glance to Jackson.

"I don't think Val quite believes it yet, but I do," he said, pointing to his arm in a sling. "It's hard not to."

"Another war wound, eh, Charlie?" Jackson said. "Worth it though, I'd say. You both stopped Blake Harlow from killing anymore people."

That sentiment stung Valerie inside. She thought of Helen and Fred Ramirez, their bodies cut and stabbed to death by Harlow.

We weren't quick enough.

"I don't know. It just, there's something about this that reminds me of the Clawstitch killer," Valerie said, grimacing. "We never caught him."

"But you *have* caught Blake," said Jackson. "I know the fact the Clawstitch case was taken off you is a sore point, Valerie. But you must learn to let it go. I think it was a case of coming too soon for you. I'm certain the team allocated to it now are chasing him down as we speak. And surely, catching a killer of Blake Harlow's pedigree is enough to banish any dispersion that was cast about your abilities?"

"It just feels unfinished. Just like then," Valerie said. "I can't help but feel we're missing something big. The Clawstitch killer killed again because I made mistake, Jackson. What if there's more to this case and people are still in danger? I'm not sure I could handle making two fatal mistakes."

"This Clawstitch killer business does intrigue me, Valerie," interjected Will. "If you don't mind, I'd love to take a look at your notes at some point. Perhaps I could give a fresh perspective on it?"

"Sure, Will," Valerie said. "But don't you feel it? In your gut? Blake's caught, but something doesn't sit right?"

"I can't say I do, Valerie. But then, I'm not field expert. That's your realm. I'm merely here to offer an academic perspective."

"Will here has been a big help to us, Chief," Charlie said pointing to the psychologist next to him.

"Absolutely," Jackson said. "I've admired your work for some time, Doctor Cooper, and I can see that you're going to be a substantial asset here."

"Thank you," said Will. But he seemed distracted. He was watching Valerie. She smiled back at her three colleagues, but she couldn't hide the discomfort of it all.

"Valerie, are you okay?" Will asked.

"I... I am... But this case still doesn't feel right to me and it's an itch I have to scratch."

Jackson sighed loudly. "Don't try to second guess yourself, Agent Law."

There's that criticism again, she thought.

"Second guessing is a good thing, sometimes," she finally said.

"Only when something's wrong," added Charlie. "Lighten up, Val. We did it. It's been hard. But we caught the bastard."

"Yeah," she replied.

Will walked over to her. "Val, you did something wonderful today. He won't kill again. You did it."

Valerie looked up at Will. "*We* did it, Will. And you've been so much help with your insights. But you didn't see Blake before he was arrested. He was totally confused. The past, the present, they were combined. A complete temporal psychosis.

"Hmmm," Will said, rubbing his chin. "Temporal psychosis. That is rare."

"Why do I get the feeling I'm not going to like this?" Jackson said, the smile now well and truly gone from his face. "What's temporal psychosis?"

131

"It's when a person's psyche is so fractured," explained Will, "that time merges. The walls between the past and present collapse. One minute they are lucid about the time in which they live, the next they can't understand why things have changed."

Valerie walked over to Jackson. "Here me out, Boss."

"Oh, God...," Jackson rubbed his forehead and sighed again, his shoulders slumping. "Okay. Hit me with it."

"Blake Harlow couldn't understand why his adopted parents didn't still live in that house," she elaborated. "It was as if time had stood still. He got confused, and in his confusion, he had a fear response. That resulted in poor Helen and Fred Ramirez being killed."

"He's a cold, emotionless psychopath, Valerie."

Valerie could tell when Jackson was frustrated. He dropped the use of "Agent" as a professional courtesy and started using first names.

"I would agree for the most part," Will interjected.

Charlie stepped forward. "I know I shot down Val's theory about Blake being an impulse killer rather than calculating, but she's right here. I saw him. I heard him. He was completely confused."

"He could be putting it on," offered Will. "Just like the case I told you about. David Bannister, pulling the wool over everyone's eyes to manipulate everyone."

"Then give Blake Harlow an Oscar, Will," said Charlie.

"You didn't see him, Will," Valerie said. "He wasn't acting."

"David Bannister made a lot of people, even me, for a time, think he was completely impaired mentally." Will explained. "What's to say that Blake Harlow isn't doing the same to you?"

Valerie couldn't believe it. It wasn't that she was incapable of making mistakes, she'd made them before and would again in the future, but Blake Harlow had appeared so desperate, so unhinged.

"I'm following my gut on this one," she said. "I don't see how someone experiencing temporal psychosis could have so easily escaped from the Culver Institute. He seems too broken for such an ingenious escape. The planning, the foresight, it doesn't add up. I just wonder if we're breaking new ground here. A serial killer with a brand-new psychopathy we've never quite seen. Or at least one that hasn't been described in the literature."

"I will give you," said Will. "The temporal psychosis is interesting. But I'd need more to be convinced."

"Even if I'm wrong and people aren't still in danger, if we could understand him better, we might have a good chance at stopping anyone like him in the future, and even getting through to him enough to find the remains of his other alleged victims from the past," Valerie mused.

Deep down, it was more than that. She felt the entire case was wrong. She felt she'd missed something. Something big. And that didn't sit well with her. In her bones she felt that more death would follow.

Jackson looked at his team. "Charlie, what do you think?"

Charlie smiled at Valerie. "I'm with Val on this one. There's something off here about Blake Harlow's profile. It wouldn't hurt to dig a little deeper, either to understand him or double check he really did kill all the victims."

"Well, I'll side with you then, Doctor Cooper for a case well understood and finished," Jackson said. "That's two against two."

"There is a way to settle this," Valerie suggested.

"And what might that be?" asked Jackson.

"Let me interview him again. I think I can find out more."

CHAPTER TWENTY FIVE

Valerie and Blake Harlow stared at each other. They were divided by a row of jail cell bars in the basement of the Mesmer building. But the cold iron bars didn't seem enough.

Valerie was rarely unnerved by prisoners, but Harlow was different. He'd nearly killed her and Charlie just a few hours before, and the trail of bodies he'd left in his wake had gotten under Valerie's skin like few cases ever had.

Blake was sitting on the edge of a single bed. There were no sheets, nothing he could harm himself with; the agents who carried him in had made certain of that.

His shoulder was bandaged up heavily, his hand strapped to his chest, but he could be deadly even with one hand.

Valerie could hear the buzz of the fluorescent bulb above. It lit the stark environment harshly and cast downward shadows all around.

She took a breath. She steadied herself.

I'm right about you, Blake, she thought. *I'm certain of it.*

Valerie was using an old interview technique that sometimes worked with psychopaths, if they had extreme narcissistic tendencies. She would wait for him to speak first.

But he didn't. For several minutes they looked at each other. Valerie focused, Blake Harlow occasionally looking to his side as if he'd seen something out of the corner of his eye.

Finally, Valerie had to change tact and break the silence.

"Hello, Blake. Do you remember me?"

Blake shook his head from side to side. "Where am I? Where's my mom?"

"What's the last thing you remember, Blake?"

Blake's eyes darted from side to side. He shook his head as if unable to answer and then furiously slapped his forehead in anger.

"People in Mom and Dad's house," he finally said, looking up at Valerie. "They shouldn't have been there! They... shouldn't have..."

"What happened in there, Blake? I saw the bodies." Valerie wanted to know exactly what he could remember. Was he culpable for his actions?

"Are they okay?" he said, his voice wavering.

The bloodied, open-eyed faces of Helen and Fred Ramirez flashed before Valerie's eyes. That was an image now forever ingrained.

Does he really not know? Is this an act?

"They're dead, Blake. You killed them."

There was no reaction now. His pained expression suddenly melted away and became more docile, blank and cold.

"I thought so," he said in an almost mono-tonal voice. "I remember stabbing the woman through the back. I think I must have pierced her heart. She let out a gasp and then fell to the floor. I then pulled her body back into the living room so she could be with her husband."

Valerie was stunned.

There it was. He was confessing. Jackson Weller would be happy. He'd brush off Valerie's worries as an afterthought.

But something still didn't add up to Valerie. Blake was switching so quickly between emotionally cold and overwhelmed that she still felt he was too erratic to have pulled off his escape.

There's more to this, Valerie thought. *I need to go over his victims with him. Something will come. I know it.*

"You moved Mrs. Ramirez so she could be with her husband?" Valerie asked, still searching. "Why? Wasn't he already dead?"

"No, not really," Blake said. "He was badly hurt, but I didn't put the knife in his throat until I'd brought his wife's body next to him."

"What were you feeling when you brought Helen back through?"

Blake stood up from the bed and took a slow step towards the bars.

Valerie tried not to react, but she could feel her eyelids flicker slightly in apprehension.

"I thought they should be together," Blake said. "It felt wrong for them to be apart. Even though they shouldn't have been there, I didn't mean for this to happen."

Valerie felt he was starting to crack. He was showing places in his psychological defenses where she could probe.

Temporal psychosis, she thought. *I need to break through his walls to find the truth.*

Valerie felt that he was on the verge of another psychotic break. She'd have to tread carefully, push just enough to find an inconsistency that might be a path to the truth.

"It was their home, Blake," Valerie said. "You haven't lived there since you were a teenager."

135

"No, that... That can't be right...," he shook his head from side to side, the fluorescent light casting shadows around. "Mom and Dad live there with Arthur."

"Your brother is in his forties now, Blake," Valerie explained. "Your dad, you know where your dad lives, you were seen prowling around his house before you went to the orphanage and killed Miss Armstrong."

A look of shock came over Blake.

"I forgot about that... Wasn't that a dream?"

"No, Blake," Valerie answered. "It wasn't. You killed her. How does that make you feel?"

A smile crept across his face. "Happy. She can't hurt any of the other children there now."

Valerie was puzzled by Blake's answers. He was switching between showing empathy and showing psychopathic traits. A mind so inconsistent, her training wouldn't cover it. She'd have to rely on her instincts.

She decided to push his buttons further to see what would be revealed.

"You killed Miss Armstrong just like your mother," she said. "It's almost like you hated them both."

Blake fell to his knees and began to sob into his hands. "I get these terrible thoughts... The child in me comes out... It takes over... I didn't want to kill my mom, but the thoughts wouldn't let me go." His face turned to anger as he looked up, his eyes filled with tears. "But Miss Armstrong deserved it!" His voice became a loud growl.

"No one deserves that, Blake. Not Miss Armstrong, not your mother, not Mr. Stanley..." Now was the time for Valerie to show her hand. She had to know more about his escape. "And not the guards at the Culver Institute. What about them? Did you enjoy killing them?"

Blake leaped to his feet and rushed towards the bars. He slammed against the metal, and as his one free hand flailed through the bars at Valerie, she jumped back.

Two guards came rushing down the corridor towards the cell.

"It's okay," she said loudly. "Please, go back to your posts."

Blake pressed his face between the bars, grinning wide.

"I didn't kill the guards," he snarled. "Don't you put that on me!"

This admission felt too real. It felt tinged with regret. To Valerie, he sounded almost like he wanted to tell her something but was holding back.

"Then who killed the guards?"

"I... I can't say, but it wasn't me! I promise!"

"The only thing I can promise you, Blake," Valerie said. "Is that you'll never kill again."

She turned and began to walk away from the cell, her footsteps echoing between the cold floor and walls.

"Don't you put that on me!" Blake screamed. "Don't you dare!"

His screams and pounding fist against the metal bars faded into the back of Valerie's mind like a distant dream. One uncomfortable observation dominated her thoughts.

He admitted to the rest of the killings. Why not the guards?

Entering an elevator. The doors closed, completely blocking any view of the cells. As it ascended through the Mesmer building, Valerie closed her eyes and thought.

She saw images of Blake the murderer, Blake the brutal killer, but Blake the escape artist? It still didn't fit. Valerie wondered about something. A thought that seemed too terrible to embrace wholeheartedly.

The doors to the elevator pinged open.

"There you are!" a voice said from the corridor. It was Charlie. "I was just coming to get you."

He seemed concerned.

"What's wrong?" Valerie asked.

"We just got off the phone with Blake's dad," Charlie said grimly. "When I told him Blake was in custody, he was relieved. But when I asked him to tell Arthur, he seemed confused."

Valerie felt dread wash over her. She knew what was coming.

"Val, the night we spoke with Arthur Harlow and watched him drive off to look after his father... He never reached him. And his dad... He's distraught. He thinks something terrible has happened to his son."

CHAPTER TWENTY SIX

This time it was Valerie who entered Arthur Harlow's property first. The gate opened with ease, the yard perfectly kept as it had been days before.

To the eye, nothing had changed, but to Valerie, the place wasn't as picturesque as it had been. Something bubbled underneath. Worms in the soil, writhing around like the thoughts in her head.

Charlie and Will walked closely behind Valerie. As they reached the porch, Charlie pointed to the window. This time Arthur wasn't nervously calling out from it. The glass was dark, the interior cast in shadow.

Valerie knocked on the door, but nothing stirred inside. She banged again with her fist, the agitation growing inside.

What's happened to you Arthur?

She hoped that he'd just had second thoughts and returned home rather than checking in on his dad. But she feared the worst. A horrible truth was making itself known to Valerie.

There's a second killer, she thought. *Someone who helped Blake escape. Someone who could be calculating, while Blake was impulsive.*

"What do you think's happened to Arthur?" Charlie asked quietly.

"He never made it to his dad's," Valerie observed. "I keep coming back to him driving off in that car."

"What do you mean?" Charlie was looking through one of the darkened ground floor windows to see if anyone was home.

"Charlie," she said. "What if someone was hiding in the back seat?"

"Who? Blake?"

"Maybe," Valerie said. "But given his fractured mind, I'm not sure he could have stayed calm and hidden."

Charlie stepped back from the window and looked at his partner in the darkness.

"If it wasn't Blake, then who?"

"I don't know," Valerie answered. "But the more I think about this case, the more I think there's someone else involved. I'd hate to think they were hidden in that car and stopped Arthur from getting to his father's home."

Valerie tried the door handle, but it was locked. She looked at Charlie with a furrowed brow.

"You know we don't have a search warrant, right?" Charlie said, clearly understanding what Valerie was wanting to do.

"Maybe we heard something inside."

"Agreed." Charlie moved over to the door and then kicked it with great force. The door quivered but remained shut. "Arthur has this place locked up like Fort Knox."

Valerie moved to the side of the house and saw a trash can cozily nestled in a pristine enclosure. She grabbed the trash can and pulled it below a window as Charlie looked on. Then, she climbed up onto it, pulled out her flashlight, and struck the glass with it.

The window shattered. Valerie smashed the remaining shards embedded in the wooden frame.

"Be careful," Charlie whispered.

Valerie climbed inside, careful not to scratch herself on the broken glass.

She clicked her flashlight on and then helped Charlie inside.

"Feels a little different in the dark, doesn't it?" Charlie observed. "What are we looking for?"

"I'm not sure," Valerie said. But her instincts were telling her that there was something to be found in Arthur's house.

"Eh, excuse me?" a whispered voice came from outside the window. "Are you two forgetting about me?"

It was Will, and he cut an anxious figure outside in the darkness. Charlie and Valerie helped him in as he struggled on top of the trash can and then lost his balance in the window frame.

He crashed to the floor.

"Are you okay?" Valerie asked. "Did you hurt anything?"

"Just my pride." He dusted himself off.

"Wait a minute," Charlie said, pointing his flashlight to the corner of the front room.

"What is it?" asked Will.

"The motion sensors didn't go off," explained Charlie. "Val and I saw them the last time we were here. Arthur was terrified of his brother turning up. Now, why wouldn't they be on?"

"Unless they were for show," Will said, his voice hushed.

"Something is definitely off here," Valerie said stepping forward, the beam of her flashlight striking the floor ahead of her.

They moved together, three nervous investigators observing the silence of Arthur's house.

"You know," Will said. "It strikes me that Arthur might possess some of Blake's personality quirks.

"It may be a bit premature to paint him with the same brush," Charlie said.

"Normally I'd agree, Charlie," added Valerie. "But we now have two strange facts about Arthur. The first is that he never met with his father after speaking with us like he said he was going to. The second is the disabled security system and the house."

Together they entered the dining room. Valerie looked around her. It was pristine. Nothing was out of place. She turned to her colleagues.

"It's not unheard of for siblings to possess psychopathic traits. This is especially true when there's been childhood trauma."

"Exactly my thinking," said Will. "Arthur has undergone many of the same formative experiences as Blake, so it's highly unlikely that he could have been subjected to such torturous events without some form of mental health issue."

"That's a pretty big leap to psychopath, though," said Charlie.

"That's true," agreed Valerie. "We'll have to proceed under the assumption that Arthur is currently a missing person." She turned to Charlie. "Put out the word looking for Arthur; let's see if local law enforcement come across his car."

As Charlie radioed in Valerie's message, Will looked deep in thought.

"You okay, Will?" she asked.

Will didn't answer, not at first. He was too engrossed in something. Valerie followed his line of sight and noticed a painting hanging on the wall.

"I know that painting," said Will. "It's called Mother's Ruin." He stepped forward towards. "Can I borrow your flashlight please, Valerie?"

Valerie handed it to him wondering what was so interesting about the painting.

The picture depicted a woman standing drinking a large green bottle of alcohol. Behind her, a baby slept in its cot as a wolf, unbeknownst to the mother, was about to devour the child.

"Mother's ruin was a name for gin during the Victorian era," will said. "There was an epidemic of alcoholism back then in England. It was a popular thought at the time, that young mothers were abandoning their children in favor of alcohol, consumed by their addiction."

Charlie finished his call. He stepped over to his two colleagues. "What's going on?"

"I'm not sure," said Valley. "Will?"

"Look closely at the mother's face in the picture," said Will, gravely.

"My God," said Valerie moving closer to the painting. "She's missing an eye."

"This is a reproduction," said Will. "I've seen this painting many times before. Academic friend of mine who specializes in British history, has the very same reproduction on his wall. The mother's eyes in that picture are intact. Someone has gouged out the eye from this painting, quite deliberately."

"Arthur and Blake's mother… The biological mother," Valerie said. "Do you think she was an alcoholic? Could that have been why the boys were put up for adoption?"

"It's entirely possible," said Will. "This disfiguring of the picture, it's subtle. You wouldn't notice it if you haven't seen it before."

"That suggests suppressed violent thoughts," Valerie mused. "But then Arthur wouldn't be the first adopted kid to have issues with his biological mother."

Valerie turned to Charlie, but he wasn't looking at her or Will. He was leaning down and staring at the feet of an antique chest of drawers. "I think Arthur is hiding quite a lot," he said. "Look at the scuff marks on the floor. This chest of drawers has been pulled out and put back repeatedly over time."

Charlie stood up and then pulled the chest of drawers out.

Valerie gasped. Behind it was a small hole in the wall.

"Now, what do you think he's been keeping in there?" said Charlie.

"Only one way to find out," said Valerie. Stepping over to the wall, she put on some latex forensics gloves from her pocket, and then put her hand inside the hole. She rummaged around for a moment until her fingertips touched something in the darkness. It felt like a book. Valerie pulled it out.

She opened it up, and stared at what was a scrapbook, filled with drawings and notes dating back decades. The erratic though talented sketches of a women over and over again in some of the pages. On the final page, was an address, and under that the words "HIS justice cometh and soon".

Valerie pointed to the words, showing Will and Charlie.

"I believe that's directly from the Bible," said Will.

"Wait," Charlie said, shaking his flashlight back into the hole in the wall. "There's something else in here." He put his hand into the darkness. Reaching in further and further, he had to push right back into the cavity up to his shoulder. "Got it."

"Looks like you were right, Val," Charlie said staring down at what was in his hands. "There is more to this case than just Blake,"

Charlie turned and showed what he had in his hands. It was a bloodied guard's uniform. An ID badge read "Culver Institute."

"He killed the guards," Will said, stunned. "And let his brother out. But why?"

Valerie turned and looked at the painting on the wall again. The mother abandoning her baby in pursuit of her next fix. She looked at the eye, gouged out no doubt by the point of a knife. Then, thoughts formulated in a hurricane of epiphany.

"Arthur deliberately let Blake out," said Valerie, her voice almost trembling. "Arthur killed the guards and then hid somewhere on Ward 11. Blake murdered Dr. Winters, then, with his brother's help, a man capable of planning and executing such an escape in a way Blake never could... He let his brother out into the night."

Valerie touched the bloodied guard's uniform in Charlie's hands.

"He'd have known the layout of the place," said Charlie. "He did tell is that he visited before."

"Yes," Valerie answered. "And I have the feeling he's been playing us all along. Just like your David Bannister case, Will."

"Putting on a show...," said Will, now on the same page.

"Exactly," she replied. "Oh he was so clever!" She let out a pained smile. "Arthur told us all about how Blake used two boys' schoolyard fight as a cover for his own perverted games.

"The fire at the reform school?" asked Charlie.

Valerie nodded regretfully.

"Yes," she continued. "He told us Blake set one boy's bed on fire knowing that everyone would think it was to do with the fight... I bet Arthur couldn't help tell us that story. I bet it was him in the first place who set that fire. He was telling us about his crimes for his own satisfaction."

"But then he cut Blake loose after the escape," Will said. "If his primary goal was to break his brother out of there, why did he then just come home and act as if nothing had happened? Surely he would have hidden his brother away somewhere to protect him?"

Valerie held up the scrapbook in her hand. "Not if Arthur is the far more devious of the two Harlow brothers. What if Arthur didn't care about his brother escaping, but instead wanted to use him as an inverted alibi?"

"Do you mean as a cover?" asked Charlie.

"Exactly!" Valerie said, half in jubilation, half in horror. "Arthur could have orchestrated the escape of his brother, knowing that Blake would go on a murderous rampage. I wouldn't be surprised if during his visits with Blake, Arthur had planted the scenes in his mind for revenge against Miss Armstrong and the others. Hell, he might even have written a list for him. He's been doing this his entire life, manipulating his brother's more erratic psychosis to cover up his own more calculating one. Hiding his own symptoms like David Bannister did, fooling everyone, including us."

"So, let me get this straight," interjected Will. "While Blake is being blamed for every murder connected to him, Arthur can get away with another murder? One that would be blamed on his only brother?"

"But then other than the guards, which of the murder victims was killed by Arthur and not Blake?" Asked Charlie.

Valerie opened the back page of the scrapbook in her hands and showed it again. "This address," she said pointing at it. "And the words about justice, I think they'll lead to Arthur's intended victim. The person Arthur wants to kill most in the world. We haven't found that person yet."

Charlie looked up at the painting on the back wall. "You don't think…"

Valerie stared at her to colleagues with grim determination. "Arthur is going to kill his biological mother." She rushed back towards the window and began climbing out, a cold dread washing over her that they might already be too late.

CHAPTER TWENTY SEVEN

Elmira Phillips had gone to bed early fearing for her life. This fear had grown like a cancer in her mind for days. Little things had helped her to maintain a sense of security, but only just. The windows locked. The door double bolted. And the knife sitting comfortably beneath her pillow.

She'd even practiced putting a hand underneath her head and pulling the knife out quickly should her attacker come.

The local news had been full with reports of Blake Harlow escaping from a secure psychiatric ward and going on a bloody killing spree. Elmira knew that name well. When Blake had originally been arrested for murdering his adopted mother, Elmira had been informed by a psychiatrist.

She didn't remember the psychiatrist's name; everything about him was gray and innocuous. But she never forgot those words "I'm afraid your son is a killer." The psychiatrist had told her that Blake's fragmented mind and psychopathic tendencies came from unresolved issues regarding his childhood. If only she would speak with him, perhaps he would open up, and perhaps he would tell authorities about any other suspected victims.

But Elmira had long since cut those ties. She cut them when she gave up her two sons, knowing that she could no longer look after them.

When the reports of Blake's escape did the rounds, she instinctively feared what he would do to her if he found her. After all, he had already killed his adopted mother; it made sense to her that she would be on his list. And fate had played its better hand by placing the Culver Institute only a few miles from the cozy home in which she now lay.

Sleep would not come. Thoughts raged in her mind. She waited for the sound of broken glass. The window being pulled up, and the grinning, malevolent face of her son climbing into her house.

But it had been a few nights, and this had not happened. An uneasy truce in her weird mind was beginning to formulate. Perhaps she was safe. Perhaps he had been caught.

Staring at the clock by her bedside was intolerable. She decided that she would get up and make yourself a nice cup of hot cocoa. Leaving the room behind, she walked into her kitchen.

A drawer was lying open, cutlery inside of it.

She didn't remember leaving it open. But she had been under immense stress. Anxiety played tricks with memory.

Elmira closed the drawer and reached for her favorite cup hanging from a peg beneath several fitted cupboards.

She placed the cup down on top of the worktop, and it clinked slightly. But as it did, she thought she heard another sound joining it.

She moved her head slightly to the side to listen, her hair standing up on the back of her neck.

There it was again. Sort of a shuffling sound. Like someone dragging their feet.

"Hello?" she said nervously to the empty kitchen doorway.

The sound came again. Another shuffle. Was it a rustling sound? Like someone moving and their clothing making an almost imperceptible sound.

Elmira took a deep breath, and it swallowed slightly. She always did that when she was nervous. She had since she was a child.

When the sound came a third time, she looked to the kitchen block where her knives sat. Pulling one out, she cursed herself for leaving her cell phone by her bed.

Stepping forward towards the doorway, she hoped and prayed that it was not her returning son. The son she once abandoned. A son intent on revenge.

Slowly she moved through the doorway into the hall. She then heard the sound of cloth again, this time with the padding noise following.

"I've... I've got a knife...," she said unconvincingly. Yes, she had a knife, but would she know how to use it?

The noise had come from the bathroom. The door was slightly ajar, obscuring the view. She swallowed nervously again and decided to take a look. Pushing the door open with her hand, it creaked slightly.

Elmira let out a palpable sigh of relief.

On the floor of the bathroom was a pile of towels. Elmira remembered leaving them on top of an already brimming laundry basket the night before, after work. She'd been too tired to put them away.

The towels had slipped off the pile by themselves and landed on the

145

floor.

But what about the other shuffling noises? she thought.

Probably fell one by one. That's it. No need to panic, Elmira.

She went back to the kitchen and composed herself. She had to get over this fear of her son coming for her. They'd catch him sooner or later, but what if it took time? Days, weeks, months? The thought of years of fearing for her life did not sit well with Elmira. Not after the years she'd already wasted as an alcoholic, consumed by self-doubt and self-pity in equal measure.

She'd have to live with the thought of Blake being out there somewhere, just as she'd learned to live with the regret of abandoning him and Arthur as kids.

Elmira put the knife back in the wooden block and made a cup of warm cocoa. It was soothing. She then sat in front of the TV in the living room. First, she put on the news. But when a breaking report came on about Blake Harlow, escaped killer, she reached for the remote.

"Blake Harlow," the reported on the television said, "has been arrested and is now in custody."

Elmira let out a sigh of relief. It was over. She would be safe.

Thank God, she thought.

She watched intently as the reporter delved deeper into how he was caught.

"It's believed that Harlow was arrested during a dramatic fight with two FBI agents," the reporter continued. "Known for several violent murders, including butchering the head mistress of Bristlewood Orphanage, experts are speculating about what could drive a man to viciously execute an elderly lady. We're now joined by psychologist Bill Freeman who is here to give his thoughts on Blake Harlow's crimes, and how his family life may be at the center of his evil attacks."

Elmira felt the old guilt wash over her. She changed the channel to something less harrowing.

Reruns of Cheers often played that late at night, and so she sat and watched an episode as she sipped her hot chocolate, trying to forget her worries.

When the cup was finished and the episode concluded, Elmira got up feeling suitably groggy and ready for a good night's sleep. She put the cup back in the kitchen and then went to her bedroom.

Climbing underneath the covers, she felt the security of the blankets. A memory came to her, of being tucked in by her father when

146

she was a kid. It was a nice one. One of the few she had of him.

She let out a sigh and allowed herself to sink deep into the comfortable mattress and pillow.

Just before sleep took her, Elmira reached for another comfort. She put her hand underneath the pillow to make certain that the knife was still there.

It wasn't.

Someone had taken it.

That was when Elmira Phillips opened her eyes to the sound of a creak by her bedroom door. It slowly opened, and from the shadows, a man stood staring at her from the darkness. He moved forward quickly.

Elmira barely had a chance to scream.

CHAPTER TWENTY EIGHT

"Out of the way!" Valerie yelled from the passenger window as her frustrations boiled over.

A delivery truck parked in front of their car. She brandished her FBI shield, but the driver looked around in bemused fashion as though he had no inkling of where he could move his vehicle.

"Charlie....," Valerie said, turning to her partner behind the wheel.

"Detour?" said Charlie.

"Detour," answered Valerie, knowingly.

"What detour?" said Will from the backseat, nervously.

"Hold on to your degrees, Will," Charlie said as he stomped on the gas and hurtled towards the delivery car.

"You're going to crash!" Will shouted.

At the last moment, Charlie swerved and mounted the sidewalk. The curb clunked against the underside of the car as something grated against the concrete.

The car hurtled along the empty sidewalk before swerving back onto the road. The traffic surrounding the car appearing like a swarm of bees to Valerie. But they had to get through it.

Screeching around a corner, Valerie pointed to one of several picturesque houses.

"There!"

Charlie slammed on the breaks.

"Wait here, Will," Valerie ordered.

"Gladly," Will said, looking like he was going to be sick.

Charlie and Valerie rushed from the vehicle, drawing their guns and reaching the door of the house.

Charlie slammed his fist against the door. "FBI! Open up!"

Valerie didn't wait for an answer. She had to save the mother. That drive streamed through her veins. She stepped back.

"We don't have time."

She then shot at the locks, the sound of wood splintering, echoing out and down the street.

With one solid front kick, the door almost came off of its hinges.

"Wait! Val! Slowly!" Charlie said.

But Valerie didn't wait, as if the life of her own mother were at stake.

She rushed into the darkened hallway inside.

"Arthur!" she yelled.

Gun raised and arm extended, Valerie swept the rooms, Charlie urging her to slow down.

"You're going to get killed acting like this," he whispered over her shoulder.

"Arthur!" she yelled again, ignoring Charlie's advice.

With each room she entered, she said "clear," but when they entered a bedroom, what they found stopped them in their tracks.

Sitting in a rocking chair was the sheet white figure of a woman of almost 60. Her white night dress was covered in blood, her face heavily bruised, and her eyes were wide and pleading.

In her lap lay the much larger figure of Arthur.

The mother rocked back and forward, back and forward, each time the chair letting out an unsettling creak. Her exposed arms were covered in dark bruises. And all the while, Arthur had a knife pointing up to his biological mother's throat.

"Keep rocking," he said in an infantile voice.

The sound of a man in his 40s mimicking that of a young boy made Valerie feel sick to her stomach. It was an unnatural bastardization of the mother child relationship.

The woman continued to stare at the two FBI agents, her eyes begging them to do something and stop the torture.

"Arthur," Valerie said firmly. "We know you killed the guards. We know you let your brother out to cover your tracks. This has gone too far, but it needn't end worse."

Arthur began to sob, his voice still aping that of a child.

"No, no, no, I want my Mommy," he said, nestling his head against the woman's bloodied chest, while never taking his knife from her throat.

Valerie's stomach churned at that plea. The mask had indeed slipped, revealing Arthur's infantile desires.

"Arthur," Valerie continued. "If you put the knife down, will get you the help you need."

"I... I don't want to."

"What is it that you do want?"

Arthur turned his head and looked directly at Valerie. "I want my mommy, and if I can't have that...," Arthur's face turned into a sneer. A rage filled snarl. "Then she can pay for what she's done to me. To us."

Valerie needed to get into Arthur's head. She didn't want to. She didn't want to use the immersion technique in such a precarious situation. But she had no choice. Any hesitation could result in the knife been plunged up through Arthur's mother's throat and at the back of her neck.

And so she let him in.

She let his scheming, his manipulation of his brother, his hidden psychopathy - all of it came in, a tsunami of warped ideas and desires. All to get close to his mother.

Comfort, Valerie thought. *This is about comfort, not killing.*

Valerie was sure of it: Arthur wanted to get back to a simpler time, he wanted to be with his mother, be cared for and protected. But the mother's abandonment was a permanent hurdle to that place. It could only be broken down by blood-covered, brutal affection. A violent act mixed with love and hate as Arthur sat in his mother's arms, reverting to the childlike personality that had lay hidden from view all these years.

The kill is a twisted embrace.

A flash came to Valerie. She had a way in. At least a way to stay his hand, if he listened. A connection.

"I haven't seen my mother for years, Arthur," Valerie could feel Charlie tensing up beside her, unsure of what she was doing.

Arthur looked at her puzzled.

She continued, "When I was barely a teenager, she had a complete breakdown. She had delusions about me and my younger sister being possessed with some sort of evil. She had to cut it out from us. That it was the only way to save our mortal souls."

Arthur appeared transfixed by Valerie's words. If she was letting who he was into her mind, then he was doing the same. A sharing of experiences. A sharing of words carrying pain and misery with them.

"She wanted to start cutting my sister first," Valerie said. "But I had to protect my sister. I managed to persuade my mother to let my sister go into another room. I whispered to my sister that she should get help. Then it was me alone with my mother. I remember hearing the latch on the door slightly as my sister fled the apartment. I was glad that she was out of harm's way, but I was certain that my own mother was about to kill me. Though her intentions were good, her mind was so fractured that she saw something in me that wasn't there. An evil that had to be

150

removed like a malignant cancer.

"So I protected my sister. I got this for my troubles." Valerie pulled her sleeve back. It revealed a several deep scars running up along her skin.

Arthur was mesmerized as his mother continued to rock him back and forth.

Valerie stared at Arthur. "My mother hurt me, too. But she didn't know what she was doing. I have to forgive her, even if the pain of that day will never go away. Because the pain will eat away at you and leave nothing behind but misery. I carry that pain inside, and sometimes, just sometimes, I want to both love *and* hurt her."

"I...," Arthur hesitated. "I have to *kill* mommy."

"No, Arthur," Valerie said, lowering her gun. She stepped forward. "You don't have to kill anyone. Don't you see? We're the same, you and me. The same. Our mothers mistreated us, they abandoned us, but we don't have to be *like* them. We can choose to be different. Please, today is your day. Choose to be different. Choose to embrace life, not snuff it out."

Tears filled Arthur's eyes as he lowered the knife. "I can't do this." His voice was back to its normal register.

Then his mother finally spoke. "I'm... I'm sorry, Arthur. I didn't mean to leave you. I couldn't cope... I had to give you up for a better life."

Arthur shook his head. "Better for you or us?"

"For all of us."

"No, no...," Arthur began to strike his head with his hands. His voice then suddenly raised up in pitch again. A child in a man's body. "Here, Mommy. Let's sing together."

Arthur thrust the knife upward towards his mother's throat.

Valerie raised her gun, but Charlie got a shot off first. It struck Arthur in the shoulder. He yelped in pain. An animalistic scream that soon turned to rage.

He threw the knife at Charlie.

Charlie ducked out of the way as the knife lodged itself in the wall behind.

Valerie pulled her trigger, but it was too late. Arthur was grasping for it. The gun went off again, the bullet embedding in the floor.

Arthur kicked out, striking Valerie in the stomach. She dropped her gun as Arthur charged again at her. The force knocked her backwards into Charlie, who smashed his head against the doorway frame.

Reaching up with spite seething from him, Arthur pulled the knife out of the wall, powdered plaster seeping out from the slit. As Valerie and Charlie both lay dazed on the floor, he stepped over to his mother in the rocking chair and held the knife an inch from her face.

She screamed in terror.

"I'll finish our play time in a minute, Mommy," Arthur said with a blood splattered grin.

"Charlie...," Valerie groaned looking to her side. He was unconscious, blood dripping down his forehead. Fear came as she looked up at Arthur, knife in hand standing over her. A flash of her mother came to her. The same pose. Holding a knife and consumed by the desire to cut her.

Reaching out, Valerie grabbed for the gun on the floor, but Arthur anticipated this and stomped on her wrist. She felt something snap inside. Blinding pain ran up her arm. She let out a loud gasp.

Arthur leaned over and grabbed Valerie by the hair. She screamed as he dragged her across the floor.

Something then struck the back of Arthur's head. He staggered backwards, letting go of Valerie. She slumped to the ground. Arthur turned around to see a man standing behind him holding a broken vase. He didn't know it, but he was staring at Doctor Will Cooper.

Will recoiled in horror as Arthur, unperturbed, lunged towards him with his knife.

A loud bang sounded, and Arthur stumbled. Charlie was awake, dazed and concussed, but awake. Smoke rolled out of the barrel of his handgun.

Arthur cried out angrily and lunged again. Charlie groggily pulled the trigger again, but his reactions were off. Arthur swiped at the gun and pulled it from his weakened hand.

Looking at the gun in his hand with a wide, insane gaze. He grinned.

"Mommy says I shouldn't play with others."

He pointed the gun at Charlie as Valerie scrambled across the ground for her own revolver.

Another bang. Another bullet. Then another. And another. And another.

Valerie watched as four holes in Arthur's back pushed out blood like a sewer. He dropped to his knees and, then let out a slow gasp as the light flickered from his eyes and he died.

Valerie's hand was agony. She looked to her two friends, one bruised and bloodied on the floor, the other still holding a piece of broken vase, not quite sure what to do with himself.

She was glad they were on her side.

In the rocking chair, the battered and bruised Elmira Phillips, mother of Arthur and Blake Harlow, sat on the rocking chair. She was staring down at the dead body of her son and saying something over and over again under her breath.

Valerie stood up, holding her wrist, and walked over to the woman.

"It's... It's okay," she said. "We'll get you help."

But the woman didn't respond. She just stared at her dead son. Finally, Valerie recognized what she was saying under her breath. It was a nursery rhyme. The kind you would sing to soothe a young child.

CHAPTER TWENTY NINE

Valerie's skin itched like hell beneath the plaster cast. Arthur Harlow had broken her wrist in three places. It was so mangled that she required several hours of surgery to set everything correctly. That meant time off work, which was not what Valerie needed.

Worse than that, after already having sat around her apartment for three days, it was her birthday, and her boyfriend Tom was fussing.

The apartment smelled like an Italian restaurant. Tom was in the kitchen and in his element. Valerie could hear him singing "Our House," an overtly sentimental song she didn't care for. But then, she'd never had a happy house before. Not as a kid, at least.

The sound of a cork popping came from in the kitchen.

"I can't have a drink," Valerie said, still lying on the couch with a magazine in her hand. "The painkillers, remember?"

Tom appeared with a tray full of glasses.

"They're not for you," he said with a mischievous grin.

Valerie looked at the door behind him. "No, please, Tom, I'm not in the mood for visitors."

"It's your birthday, Honey," he said. "And we're celebrating two things."

"Two?" she said, melting slightly at the sight of Tom's ever optimistic and loving smile.

"Your operation being successful, and...," Tom was interrupted by a knock at the door.

He grinned and then rushed off to answer it.

In traipsed Charlie, Will, and even her boss Jackson.

"There's the wounded soldier," Charlie said in a deliberately condescending voice. He walked over and ruffled her hair like a child. "How's my big girl doing? Feeling better?"

"You know," Valerie said. "My other arm is perfectly fine. And I can aim with that one too. Tom, get my gun."

"I brought a bottle of Moet for this evening's events," said Will, handing Tom a bottle.

"Ah," said Tom. "I've just opened some champagne, but we'll

drink this second."

"Sounds like we're in for a good drinking session," said Charlie. "This I can get behind."

"Don't you have two kids and a wife at home to take care of, Charlie?" Valerie asked.

"Yes," said Charlie. "But in a stroke of genius, my wife is taking care of the kids and the kids are taking care of her."

"How very 21st century of you," Will joked.

Valerie appreciated her colleagues being jovial, but deep down she wasn't quite ready to let her hair down. She knew in their eyes that they had been affected by the case, too. But the parallels between the Harlow boys and Valerie and her own sister...

It was enough to give her sleepless nights.

So many dead. *If only I had been quicker.*

She tried not to show her true feelings.

"Boss, I'm sorry you got roped into this," she said looking up at Jackson, trying on a smile as best she could.

"Never mind about that," said Jackson. "I wanted to tell you that the final report on the Harlow case has been approved."

"Great," Valerie replied. "Did they ever figure out the exact way the brothers escaped?"

"Apparently," Charlie interjected, "Arthur used the ventilation system to get into the building unseen. He was then able to walk the corridors inside dressed as a security guard. We're still unsure how he got that, but we think he had it manufactured from pictures he took during his visits.

"Arthur had sneaked a phone into his brother's room, which Blake hid. He then told Blake when to break the camera in his room to lure the guards in. Then, once Blake was out of the ward and panic ensued, Arthur directed him over the cellphone to a closet with a vent inside that he had loosened off."

"You ought to see the security footage," added Jackson. "The timing was impressive. Arthur Harlow even misdirected two groups of guards, telling them he'd seen Blake going in a different direction. At some point, both the brothers exited the building via the vents and that was that."

"But that was your last case, Agent Law," Jackson said. "How about you get ready for your next one?"

He handed her a piece of paper.

"What is it?" Valerie said.

155

"A gift," said Jackson. "Just what you wanted."

Valerie looked down at the paper. There was much text on procedural clauses that were departmental stuff. But one line took her breath away:

Agents Valerie Law and Charles Carlson given priority access to case #85673 - The Clawstitch Killer case.

She couldn't believe it. She was being given access to the one case that had nearly ended her career. The most brutal and sadistic killer she had ever encountered, and one that was so intelligent, he had been able to manipulate the entire FBI into chasing a hundred dead ends.

This was a chance to redeem herself, though she knew that it would lead into some of the darkest places an investigator could ever go.

Valerie teared up, overwhelmed. "Did you do this, Jackson?"

"Actually," he said. "Two of us did." He pointed into the kitchen where the sound of Will recounting a stuffy joke about his college days could be heard. "The directors upstairs were extremely impressed with how you handled the Harlow brothers. And I merely inquired about the possibility of you being given access to the case.

"It turns out, the investigating agents have hit a bit of a dead end, so to speak. It's ruffled a few feathers, but after I spoke with them, Will wrote a letter of recommendation which seemed to open more doors for you. It seems one of the directors is a fan of his."

Valerie smiled looking down at the piece of paper. "Don't tell him that, it'll go to his head."

Jackson looked over his shoulder to make sure no one was coming over. He sat down and whispered.

"Do you think he'll work out then at the CPU?"

"Definitely. He has a brilliant mind. But he's brave too. He really saved our bacon at Elmira Phillips's home. Speaking of which, how is she?"

Jackson's mood became more somber "She's in the hands of a great psychiatric ward, but I fear she'll never quite be the same again. She'll be in the hospital recovering for some time."

Valerie shook her head, thinking of her own mother locked away in a ward somewhere.

Tom appeared through the doorway carrying a bottle of champagne. He began to fill the glasses on the table. "You two look glum," he said. "Don't tell me you're talking shop already."

"I've been given back the Clawstitch killer case," Valerie said enthusiastically.

156

Tom's demeanor changed. "I see."

"Eh, it's okay, Tom," Charlie said coming into the room. "It won't be the same as last time."

"Certainly not," said Will, following suit. "You'll have me with you for starters."

"Yeah," said Charlie. "We can't give him a gun, but we're thinking of arming him with a glass vase. Deadly."

"That was antique. Broke my heart to do it," said Will.

"Are you sure you know what you're doing, Val?" Tom asked

"He's the killer who got away, Tom. He nearly ended my career just as it was going somewhere. And... I need to make up for mistakes if I can. It's stuck inside of me until I do."

Tom sighed. "Sometimes I wish you were a librarian. It would be much easier."

"Plus access to great books," Will said, sipping his champagne. "That's always a bonus."

"But," said Tom, "if you think it'll get that monkey off your back, Val. Then I'm behind you."

"I do."

"You wouldn't say that in front of a preacher, would you?" Tom laughed.

"Champagne's quite enough for now, Tom," Valerie joked. "But stick around, who knows what'll happen."

Her friends laughed and joked. She did, too, as best she could. But in between the laughter, in between the smiles and companionship, Valerie saw the glances. She saw the same look from Will and Charlie that she felt too, deep in her bones.

Too many people had died at the hands of the Harlows. Future cases would come, and each of them would bring danger and damage to the world.

It was their job to stop that from happening, but when the worst did occur and someone died, Valerie felt it deeply. It was, in some way, as if a small piece of her soul perished, too.

*

The champagne had gone to all of their heads, except Valerie's. It was her birthday, and she was the only sober one between them. Her mind was still fixated on the violence they had witnessed throughout the case. Perhaps the rest could sense that.

Jackson had left the apartment first, clearly feeling a little uncomfortable with being too drunk around his staff.

Charlie was in the kitchen, regaling Tom with a story from his Army days. Tom was hearing a lot of stories, and Valerie sympathized with him. When would he get the chance to tell some of his own?

In the living room, while a Coltrane record played in the background, Will sat in an armchair across from Valerie.

"Oh, my word," he said. "I haven't drank this much in some time."

"That's what happens when you put away a killer."

"Two of them, Valerie."

"Yes, two," she repeated. "You know, part of me feels for Blake."

"How so?"

"He was so manipulated by his brother. At least Arthur had been able to live a life outside; Blake had been locked up for decades."

"True," said Will. "But you must remember, they were both killers. Even if Blake had been released as a cover for Arthur's plans, he still chose to kill the others."

"Do you ever worry that...," Valerie stopped for a second. "It's a stupid idea."

"You're thinking about Blake and Arthur's mother, aren't you?"

Valerie was surprised that Will could read her so well, especially after only having known each other for a couple of weeks. But then, people bonded over extreme situations, and the Harlow case had certainly been one of those.

"Yes," she said succinctly.

"You're wondering if Blake really was the one who killed his mother aren't you?"

"And all the bad things he did at school," Valerie wondered. "What if some of that was Arthur? What if Blake was made into a killer by his brother to cover his own crimes?"

Will sat up in his chair and let out a tired groan. "It's a thought, you know. But unless Blake confesses to that, it would be difficult to prove. With Arthur dead and Blake so fragmented that he doesn't know what's real and what's not, we may never know the full truth."

There was silence as the record reached its end and the player switched off. Charlie was still drunkenly prattling away to Tom in the kitchen. Valerie was pretty certain Tom hadn't said a word for twenty minutes.

"Valerie, I hope I'm not being forward," Will said.

Valerie tensed up, wondering what was coming next.

158

"I did hear some of what you said about your mother back at the house to Arthur Harlow... About your mother..."

"You were listening?"

"I was in the hallway. I'm sorry. I know you might not want to talk now..."

Valerie sighed. "I've carried it for so long, I'm not sure I ever want to talk about it."

Will raised an eyebrow. "What would a talented profiler think of that?"

Valerie shook her head. "That the person was repressing their trauma. That it would affect them in other ways, affect their feelings, their behaviors, their... choices."

"That would be a very insightful conclusion for a profiler to think," Will said, looking at his friend.

There was another awkward silence.

Valerie felt the sadness in it. She felt like she wanted to fill it. She wanted to tell Will about all the horrible things that had happened to her as a child.

She wanted to tell him about her mother's hallucinations, about how they drove her to harm and then to a lifetime as a permanent psych ward patient.

She wanted to tell him about how her own sister had also been in and out of institutes her whole life. About how her sister suffered deeply from bipolar disorder, and sometimes seemed just like her mother.

Most of all, she wanted to tell Will about how she felt inside. The terror that one day the same delusions that had driven her mother to violence, might make themselves known inside her own mind.

She knew that bipolar disorder didn't make a person violent, but she worried that the violence was already in her, and that any disturbance in her personality might bring it to the fore.

What would Will make of all that? she wondered.

But Valerie didn't say any of this. She just turned and heard Tom finally speak in the kitchen. Something about wanting to take her on vacation.

If I'm going to tell anyone, it should be Tom first, she thought.

The silence had outstayed its welcome. But it was Will who broke it.

"We all carry trauma, Valerie," he said. "When we face something like the Harlow case, that can spark deep self-reflection, even an

159

obsession with… comparisons." Will leaned forward slightly, staring with his soft eyes.

"You're a good person, Valerie," he said. "And if you ever want to talk about a case… Or anything else… I'll be here."

"Thanks, Will," she said. "I'm glad to know you."

"You know," he said, seemingly sensing not to push any further, "these Harlow brothers might make for an interesting book. Would you…"

Valerie laughed. "No, I'll catch them, you write about them, Will. But you're right. It's been a strange case."

"Yes, two brothers with the same exact, psychosis," he said fixing his glasses. "Both with a repressed child personality that could take over at any time, but Arthur's being far more controlled."

"I think Arthur is just as sick as Blake."

"I agree," Will said. "He probably was able to maintain his own demons by manipulating his brothers'. Who knows how two siblings end up like that?"

Valerie tried not to think of her sister. She tried not to think about *their* similarities. Could they be consumed by the same thing, too?

Another silence came. And Valerie once more did not break it. She was in too somber a mood. She was finding it difficult to pull herself away from her darkest fears.

"Are you happy about being back on the Clawstitch case?" Will asked, abruptly shaking Valerie from her thoughts.

"Yeah," Valerie said, uncertain. "I appreciate what you guys did for me."

"You seem a little unnerved by it."

"Charlie and I were supposed to be chasing down a fugitive guilty of fraud, not a killer."

"What happened?"

"Would you believe, our target became one of the killer's victims?" Valerie said shaking her head. "We were allowed to investigate because the cases overlapped, even not specializing in that sort of thing yet. But…"

"You made a mistake."

"I sent us down the wrong path," she said, sadness in her voice. "It forced all of us to look for him at a specific location; all the while, he was really in another state, killing a couple of drifters. If I hadn't gotten that wrong…"

"We all make mistakes, Valerie," Will said adjusting his glasses.

160

"You can't carry that with you wherever you go. Besides, you're getting a second bite at the apple now. That doesn't come around very often."

"I know," Valerie said. "I want to catch him and face him. But there is something you should know, between you and me. Charlie is the only other person on the planet that's heard this."

"What is it?" Will asked, sitting up straight.

"I think the Clawstitch killer might be in law enforcement, maybe a cop. He was always one step ahead of us, and the way he manipulated the chase, leading us in circles, it was as if he had intimate knowledge of police procedures. It's just a theory but..."

"Worth looking into," Will said. "I take it Jackson doesn't know this."

"If he thought I was going to insinuate that someone in law enforcement was a brutal serial killer, I think he'd have let me sit this one out." Valerie stood up and looked out of her apartment window to the darkened streets below. "But Will, he can't know. Not until we have something more to go on. I'd be kicked off the case for good after the trouble I caused last time."

"Agreed," said Will. "When do you want to start?"

"I need to let my hand heal, doctor's orders. Besides, there's something I have to do first."

"Oh, what's that?" Will asked.

Valerie looked out to the night. "Something personal. Maybe I'll tell you one day."

EPILOGUE

"Are you sure you want to do this?" Tom asked, standing with Valerie in the rain. Ealing Psychiatric Hospital loomed down on them both from above as if listening to their conversation.

"Yeah," Valerie answered after taking a moment, the rain pattering on the umbrella above them, blocking out the bleak skies overhead. "It's time."

"Okay." Tom gave Valerie a kiss on the cheek. "But if you want to leave at any point, you just say the word and we're out of here."

Valerie nodded.

Tom opened the glass door to the towering building. The smell of bleach and other cleaning products filled the air. But beneath the sterile, clinical scent was something else.

It was a smell that Valerie had noticed in most hospitals. The masking of decay.

It reminded her of her mother.

The chatter of two nurses behind the large front desk quickly ceased. They looked up.

"Can I help you?" asked one of them.

"I'm here to see Suzie Law, please." Valerie's pulse quickened at her own words. She had wanted to see her sister but had only found out that morning that she was now in a psychiatric ward.

"Name?"

"Valerie Law. I'm her sister."

"One moment," a nurse with an all-too cheery round face and disposition said.

Tom squeezed Valerie's hand in support. She squeezed back.

Picking up a phone at the desk, the nurse dialed in some numbers and then waited with the phone lodged between her ear and shoulder.

"Yes," she said. "I have a visitor for Suzie Law, can she... Oh." The nurse's jovial demeanor dipped. "I see. Okay. Thank you."

Valerie read the woman's body language. Something was wrong.

"I'm afraid there's been an incident and your sister has been moved to a secure ward," the nurse said grimly.

Valerie didn't understand. She was supposed to be stable; the doctor had told her so over the phone.

"But she only came in for a few days' treatment. Voluntarily?"

"You'll have to discuss it with the ward doctor, if you can find him." The nurse's expression softened. "Sorry for the bad news."

"It's okay," Valerie said with worry in her voice. "Which level?"

"Eight."

"Thank you." Valerie held Tom's hand and led him towards a single elevator in the lobby.

"I'm sorry," the other nurse said loudly. "But it's immediate family only. You'll have to wait here, Sir."

Tom turned around. "Now wait just a minute, my girlfriend hasn't seen her sister in years, she's only now been informed that she has deteriorated, and I can't even..."

"It's okay, Tom." Valerie loved that he would go to bat for her. But there was no point. She knew how hospitals operated, especially around their secure wards. "I'll be fine. Wait here for me. I won't be long."

"But..." Tom's deep gaze was filled with care. Valerie loved that, too.

"Why don't you tell the nurses behind the desk some of your dad jokes," she smiled.

"But I'm not a dad."

"No, you're not. But you've got the humor down." Valerie leaned in and kissed Tom on the mouth. "I'll be fine," she whispered and then entered an elevator, the doors closing behind her.

The ride up was rough, the elevator feeling decidedly lethargic as it slowly shuffled up through the building.

You and me both, Buddy, Valerie thought, still not fully recovered from the Harlow case.

Button 8 lit up, a ping came with it, and the doors opened.

The smell of bleach was now stronger. The memory it brought her was of her mother obsessed with cleaning their childhood home. The chemical smell stung in her nose and lungs.

As she stepped out of the elevator and walked along a corridor to the secure psychiatric ward, she remembered her mother's fingers bleeding as she scrubbed everything down to the bone.

That had been an early indication of her declining mental health when they had been kids. Valerie had been old enough to know something was wrong. But she had tried to protect Suzie. She told her stories to keep her mind away from the reality of their sick mother and her paranoid episodes.

Almost in a daze, Valerie showed some ID at the ward desk to another nurse. Then, the security door was opened, and Valerie stepped inside.

The irony wasn't lost on her: She had been resting after a case that started in a secure psychiatric ward, only to find herself back inside another one, but this time for personal reasons.

The ward corridor felt suffocating, and it brought with it the old fear. *My mother's sick. My sister's sick. Will I end up in a place like this?*

Valerie walked along the ward corridor with a nurse who barely spoke a word. The room doors and their tiny glass portholes were filled with the faces of other patients as they passed.

One man spat at the glass in her direction. Another screamed profanity at her. Then she saw a woman sobbing, her forehead resting against the cold glass of another secured room.

Valerie's blood ran cold.

The woman was her sister.

How has it come to this? she thought as she tentatively approached the door.

Suzie continued to sob, her voice distant behind the door.

Valerie steadied her hand as she reached up and tapped the glass.

Suzie, wide-eyed and clearly sleep deprived, recoiled away from the glass at the sight of Valerie.

"Can you let me in?" Valerie said, turning to the accompanying nurse.

"Are you sure?"

Valerie nodded.

The door was soon opened, revealing Suzie in a white hospital gown, curled up on a bed, weeping. Her blond hair drooped down over her face, her eyes glaring out from between the wild strands.

Valerie stepped inside.

"I can wait here," the nurse offered.

"That won't be necessary, thank you," Valerie said, closing the door and leaving the nurse out in the corridor

This was the first time Valerie had laid eyes on her sister for three years. When she had received the messages from her, she had been out in the world, but for the sixth time, she had now fallen back into psychiatric care.

Valerie was shocked by her disheveled appearance.

"Suzie," Valerie said softly.

Suzie looked up. "Are you really here, Val?" she whispered.

"I'm real, Suzie. I'm real."

Suzie kicked her head back forcefully and laughed at the sterile white ceiling.

"Oh, the FBI agent returns! Here to gloat at your poor little sister?"

"I'm here to help, Sis." Valerie's heart ached at the sight of her sister, still clearly in the throws of another manic episode.

"Are you here to tell me I'm mad?" Suzie said, the tears still streaming down her cheeks from behind a shroud of blond hair. "Did the doctors need you for reinforcements?"

"It's not a battle, Suzie."

"Isn't it?" she said, moving to the edge of the bed, her pale feet dangling above the cold floor. "It sure feels like it sometimes. Especially trying to get in touch with you."

"Suzie, I had no idea things had gotten this bad. I thought you were better."

"Ha! Better she says," Suzie grabbed her own left arm with her right hand. "You'll find so many pin pricks here. They've filled me full of drugs and thrown me in this room, all because I got angry with another patient for stealing my stuff."

"I didn't even know you were back in the hospital," Valerie said.

"You never asked!"

Valerie took a deep breath. She didn't want to argue. She just wanted to heal.

"Please try to understand, Suzie. It's never been about you. I've tried for the last few years to block Mom's existence out of my mind."

Valerie reached out with her hand and touched her sister's. "I know that left you…"

"Left me having to deal with her? Yeah, that doesn't quite cover it, Val. Maybe if you'd helped more, I wouldn't have had another breakdown and ended up in here!"

"I'm trying, Suzie." Valerie looked at her sister. All she could see was the little girl she'd tried to protect all those years ago.

"I made a decision," she continued, "that I had to walk away from Mom because dealing with what she did to us was too much. I didn't want that in my life anymore. The memory of it. The stain of it. I felt like if I was around her, I'd end up being like her.

"But the last thing I wanted was for you to be out of my life as well, Suzie. It just sort of happened. When you decided to stay in touch with Mom and visit her, I didn't know how best to handle that. I just felt numb. I threw myself into my job and tried to hide from anything that reminded me of her."

Suzie pulled away from her sister's hand and leaned back against the blank white wall, crossing her arms. "It shouldn't have taken God knows how many calls to get you to visit me. I guess the doctor contacted you this time?"

"It wasn't the calls or the messages, Suzie," said Valerie quietly. "Not completely."

"Then what was it?"

Valerie was silent for a moment. The image of Arthur and Blake Harlow's mother with bruises all over her arms flashed before her eyes.

Valerie rubbed her temple, a headache brewing.

"I went through some things lately, a case. It made me realize I had to get in touch with you. I've missed you."

Suzie grew angry. "Don't tell me you finally developed a conscience? You were happy enough to build a new life away from me, leaving me to pick up the pieces of our family."

"I'm so sorry, Suzie," said Valerie. "But I want to make amends. I want to help you."

Suzie shook her head. "The person you need to help is Mom."

"I'm here for you, not Mom."

"Well, you can't have me in your life if you won't help me deal with her... I want you to leave."

Valerie felt dismayed. "Please, Suzie. Let me stay and talk."

"I'm not going to suddenly play happy families with you, Sis." Suzie said, folding her arms. "The irony is, while I've stuck by Mom, *you're* the only one she wants to talk to."

"Why?" Valerie couldn't understand. She thought her mom hated her. At least, the part of her that was left in her twisted mind. She'd loved both her girls once long ago, but the illness had taken that from her and from them, robbing them of a happy childhood.

"She says there's something you need to hear," explained Suzie. "She says I wouldn't understand. Oh, but Valerie the perfect daughter, crime-fighting FBI agent, *she'd* know what she was talking about."

"What could she possibly want to say to me?" Valerie was genuinely puzzled.

"It's something about our family. Something you need to hear from her. Something she doesn't want to take to the grave." Suzie pointed to the closed room door as if directing Valerie where to go. "And she's scribbled down a bunch of nonsense on some sheets of paper for you. I can't make head or tails of it. But then, I don't have the Federal smarts, do I?"

"Please, Suzie…"

"Just…," Suzie sighed and stepped off her bed. She thrust her hand underneath the mattress and pulled out a collection of loose papers.

"Just go and see her," Suzie said, thrusting the papers into her sister's hands.

Valerie looked down at the papers. They were covered in her mother's erratic handwriting.

"If I look at these… then we can talk?" asked Valerie, looking up at her younger sister.

"Maybe. I don't know," Suzie turned to her side and nodded at thin air.

"Are you seeing things again, Suzie?" Valerie asked gently.

Suzie turned sharply and scowled at her sister.

"Don't try to treat me. Leave that to the doctors."

"I wasn't trying to treat you," said Valerie. "I was…"

"Just look at those papers, Val," said Suzie. "At least I can tell her you've looked. Maybe Mom will give me some peace and quiet, then."

"I could stay a while and…"

"Nurse!" Suzie screamed.

The door opened, revealing the same nurse who had accompanied Valerie.

"I want her out of here," Suzie said, her voice almost a scream.

Valerie stepped towards her sister with one hand outstretched.

"Suzie, I've come a long way. We can talk more."

Suzie winced as if one of her hallucinations had said something hurtful. The tears began to roll again.

"Please," she said. "Leave me be. It's better that way."

"I'm afraid if she doesn't want you here, you'll have to leave, Miss Law," the nurse said to Valerie.

Suzie turned and curled up in her bed. She sobbed into her hands facing the wall.

Valerie wanted to hug her sister and let her know everything would be okay. But Suzie didn't want that. And besides, Valerie couldn't say truthfully that it would ever be *okay* for either of them.

167

A daze took Valerie. Something had caught her eye.

She walked out of the room. The door closed. As she moved back through the ward and to the elevator, she didn't take her eyes off of her mother's papers for a second.

The scribbled words glared up at her.

Something about them was captivating.

The elevator descended and Valerie found Tom in the ground floor lobby waiting when the doors opened.

He rushed over to her looking concerned.

"Are you okay? Do you want to go home?" he asked.

Valerie looked down at the papers, re-reading the scrambled letters. But she saw the meaning behind them.

She shook her head somberly.

She needed to visit her mother.

They headed out of the building and back into the rain. A rain that threatened to wash away the walls of Valerie's sanity, and bring her face to face with a past she had tried to outrun for her entire life.

A past that could destroy her.

NOW AVAILABLE!

NO PITY
(A Valerie Law FBI Suspense Thriller—Book 2)

From #1 bestselling mystery and suspense author Blake Pierce comes book #2 in a gripping new series: the FBI has created an elite unit to target criminally-insane killers, and when a serial killer writes taunting letters to the press, FBI Special Agent Valerie Law and her elite team are summoned. But this killer is truly deranged, and with the trail soon cold, Valerie may just be the only who can enter his mind and crack the baffling case.

"A masterpiece of thriller and mystery."
—Books and Movie Reviews, Roberto Mattos (re *Once Gone*)

NO PITY is book #2 in a new series by #1 bestselling mystery and suspense author Blake Pierce.

Valerie, still reeling from the last case, is sure she sees a pattern when a second victim is discovered.

But when everything she thinks she knows with this killer turns out to be wrong, she questions her own judgement. Is she losing her touch?

Or is her far more diabolical than she thought?

After a shocking twist, then answer may just come too late.

A page-turning crime thriller featuring a brilliant and haunted new female protagonist, the VALERIE LAW mystery series is packed with suspense and driven by a breakneck pace that will keep you turning pages late into the night.

Book #3 in the series—NO FEAR—is now also available.

"An edge of your seat thriller in a new series that keeps you turning pages! ...So many twists, turns and red herrings... I can't wait to see what happens next."
—Reader review (*Her Last Wish*)

"A strong, complex story about two FBI agents trying to stop a serial killer. If you want an author to capture your attention and have you guessing, yet trying to put the pieces together, Pierce is your author!"
—Reader review (*Her Last Wish*)

"A typical Blake Pierce twisting, turning, roller coaster ride suspense thriller. Will have you turning the pages to the last sentence of the last chapter!!!"
—Reader review (*City of Prey*)

"Right from the start we have an unusual protagonist that I haven't seen done in this genre before. The action is nonstop... A very atmospheric novel that will keep you turning pages well into the wee hours."
—Reader review (*City of Prey*)

"Everything that I look for in a book... a great plot, interesting characters, and grabs your interest right away. The book moves along at a breakneck pace and stays that way until the end. Now on go I to book two!"
—Reader review (*Girl, Alone*)

"Exciting, heart pounding, edge of your seat book... a must read for mystery and suspense readers!"
—Reader review (*Girl, Alone*)

Blake Pierce

Blake Pierce is the USA Today bestselling author of the RILEY PAGE mystery series, which includes seventeen books. Blake Pierce is also the author of the MACKENZIE WHITE mystery series, comprising fourteen books; of the AVERY BLACK mystery series, comprising six books; of the KERI LOCKE mystery series, comprising five books; of the MAKING OF RILEY PAIGE mystery series, comprising six books; of the KATE WISE mystery series, comprising seven books; of the CHLOE FINE psychological suspense mystery, comprising six books; of the JESSE HUNT psychological suspense thriller series, comprising twenty four books; of the AU PAIR psychological suspense thriller series, comprising three books; of the ZOE PRIME mystery series, comprising six books; of the ADELE SHARP mystery series, comprising fifteen books, of the EUROPEAN VOYAGE cozy mystery series, comprising four books; of the new LAURA FROST FBI suspense thriller, comprising nine books (and counting); of the new ELLA DARK FBI suspense thriller, comprising eleven books (and counting); of the A YEAR IN EUROPE cozy mystery series, comprising nine books, of the AVA GOLD mystery series, comprising six books (and counting); of the RACHEL GIFT mystery series, comprising six books (and counting); of the VALERIE LAW mystery series, comprising three books (and counting); and of the PAIGE KING mystery series, comprising three books (and counting).

An avid reader and lifelong fan of the mystery and thriller genres, Blake loves to hear from you, so please feel free to visit www.blakepierceauthor.com to learn more and stay in touch.

BOOKS BY BLAKE PIERCE

PAIGE KING MYSTERY SERIES
THE GIRL HE PINED (Book #1)
THE GIRL HE CHOSE (Book #2)
THE GIRL HE TOOK (Book #3)

VALERIE LAW MYSTERY SERIES
NO MERCY (Book #1)
NO PITY (Book #2)
NO FEAR (Book #3

RACHEL GIFT MYSTERY SERIES
HER LAST WISH (Book #1)
HER LAST CHANCE (Book #2)
HER LAST HOPE (Book #3)
HER LAST FEAR (Book #4)
HER LAST CHOICE (Book #5)
HER LAST BREATH (Book #6)

AVA GOLD MYSTERY SERIES
CITY OF PREY (Book #1)
CITY OF FEAR (Book #2)
CITY OF BONES (Book #3)
CITY OF GHOSTS (Book #4)
CITY OF DEATH (Book #5)
CITY OF VICE (Book #6)

A YEAR IN EUROPE
A MURDER IN PARIS (Book #1)
DEATH IN FLORENCE (Book #2)
VENGEANCE IN VIENNA (Book #3)
A FATALITY IN SPAIN (Book #4)

ELLA DARK FBI SUSPENSE THRILLER
GIRL, ALONE (Book #1)

GIRL, TAKEN (Book #2)
GIRL, HUNTED (Book #3)
GIRL, SILENCED (Book #4)
GIRL, VANISHED (Book 5)
GIRL ERASED (Book #6)
GIRL, FORSAKEN (Book #7)
GIRL, TRAPPED (Book #8)
GIRL, EXPENDABLE (Book #9)
GIRL, ESCAPED (Book #10)
GIRL, HIS (Book #11)

LAURA FROST FBI SUSPENSE THRILLER
ALREADY GONE (Book #1)
ALREADY SEEN (Book #2)
ALREADY TRAPPED (Book #3)
ALREADY MISSING (Book #4)
ALREADY DEAD (Book #5)
ALREADY TAKEN (Book #6)
ALREADY CHOSEN (Book #7)
ALREADY LOST (Book #8)
ALREADY HIS (Book #9)

EUROPEAN VOYAGE COZY MYSTERY SERIES
MURDER (AND BAKLAVA) (Book #1)
DEATH (AND APPLE STRUDEL) (Book #2)
CRIME (AND LAGER) (Book #3)
MISFORTUNE (AND GOUDA) (Book #4)
CALAMITY (AND A DANISH) (Book #5)
MAYHEM (AND HERRING) (Book #6)

ADELE SHARP MYSTERY SERIES
LEFT TO DIE (Book #1)
LEFT TO RUN (Book #2)
LEFT TO HIDE (Book #3)
LEFT TO KILL (Book #4)
LEFT TO MURDER (Book #5)
LEFT TO ENVY (Book #6)
LEFT TO LAPSE (Book #7)
LEFT TO VANISH (Book #8)

LEFT TO HUNT (Book #9)
LEFT TO FEAR (Book #10)
LEFT TO PREY (Book #11)
LEFT TO LURE (Book #12)
LEFT TO CRAVE (Book #13)
LEFT TO LOATHE (Book #14)
LEFT TO HARM (Book #15)

THE AU PAIR SERIES
ALMOST GONE (Book#1)
ALMOST LOST (Book #2)
ALMOST DEAD (Book #3)

ZOE PRIME MYSTERY SERIES
FACE OF DEATH (Book#1)
FACE OF MURDER (Book #2)
FACE OF FEAR (Book #3)
FACE OF MADNESS (Book #4)
FACE OF FURY (Book #5)
FACE OF DARKNESS (Book #6)

A JESSIE HUNT PSYCHOLOGICAL SUSPENSE SERIES
THE PERFECT WIFE (Book #1)
THE PERFECT BLOCK (Book #2)
THE PERFECT HOUSE (Book #3)
THE PERFECT SMILE (Book #4)
THE PERFECT LIE (Book #5)
THE PERFECT LOOK (Book #6)
THE PERFECT AFFAIR (Book #7)
THE PERFECT ALIBI (Book #8)
THE PERFECT NEIGHBOR (Book #9)
THE PERFECT DISGUISE (Book #10)
THE PERFECT SECRET (Book #11)
THE PERFECT FAÇADE (Book #12)
THE PERFECT IMPRESSION (Book #13)
THE PERFECT DECEIT (Book #14)
THE PERFECT MISTRESS (Book #15)
THE PERFECT IMAGE (Book #16)
THE PERFECT VEIL (Book #17)

THE PERFECT INDISCRETION (Book #18)
THE PERFECT RUMOR (Book #19)
THE PERFECT COUPLE (Book #20)
THE PERFECT MURDER (Book #21)
THE PERFECT HUSBAND (Book #22)
THE PERFECT SCANDAL (Book #23)
THE PERFECT MASK (Book #24)

CHLOE FINE PSYCHOLOGICAL SUSPENSE SERIES
NEXT DOOR (Book #1)
A NEIGHBOR'S LIE (Book #2)
CUL DE SAC (Book #3)
SILENT NEIGHBOR (Book #4)
HOMECOMING (Book #5)
TINTED WINDOWS (Book #6)

KATE WISE MYSTERY SERIES
IF SHE KNEW (Book #1)
IF SHE SAW (Book #2)
IF SHE RAN (Book #3)
IF SHE HID (Book #4)
IF SHE FLED (Book #5)
IF SHE FEARED (Book #6)
IF SHE HEARD (Book #7)

THE MAKING OF RILEY PAIGE SERIES
WATCHING (Book #1)
WAITING (Book #2)
LURING (Book #3)
TAKING (Book #4)
STALKING (Book #5)
KILLING (Book #6)

RILEY PAIGE MYSTERY SERIES
ONCE GONE (Book #1)
ONCE TAKEN (Book #2)
ONCE CRAVED (Book #3)
ONCE LURED (Book #4)

ONCE HUNTED (Book #5)
ONCE PINED (Book #6)
ONCE FORSAKEN (Book #7)
ONCE COLD (Book #8)
ONCE STALKED (Book #9)
ONCE LOST (Book #10)
ONCE BURIED (Book #11)
ONCE BOUND (Book #12)
ONCE TRAPPED (Book #13)
ONCE DORMANT (Book #14)
ONCE SHUNNED (Book #15)
ONCE MISSED (Book #16)
ONCE CHOSEN (Book #17)

MACKENZIE WHITE MYSTERY SERIES
BEFORE HE KILLS (Book #1)
BEFORE HE SEES (Book #2)
BEFORE HE COVETS (Book #3)
BEFORE HE TAKES (Book #4)
BEFORE HE NEEDS (Book #5)
BEFORE HE FEELS (Book #6)
BEFORE HE SINS (Book #7)
BEFORE HE HUNTS (Book #8)
BEFORE HE PREYS (Book #9)
BEFORE HE LONGS (Book #10)
BEFORE HE LAPSES (Book #11)
BEFORE HE ENVIES (Book #12)
BEFORE HE STALKS (Book #13)
BEFORE HE HARMS (Book #14)

AVERY BLACK MYSTERY SERIES
CAUSE TO KILL (Book #1)
CAUSE TO RUN (Book #2)
CAUSE TO HIDE (Book #3)
CAUSE TO FEAR (Book #4)
CAUSE TO SAVE (Book #5)
CAUSE TO DREAD (Book #6)

KERI LOCKE MYSTERY SERIES

CPSIA information can be obtained
at www.ICGtesting.com
Printed in the USA
LVHW110606260422
717216LV00002B/29